Ring Around The Rosy, Not Another Ghosty

Janet McNulty

Ring Around The Rosy, Not Another Ghosty

Copyright © 2016 Janet McNulty
Cover Illustration by Robert Henry

ISBN-10: 1-941488-53-6
ISBN-13: 978-1-941488-53-9

For any who have ever felt like a complete klutz. You're not alone.

Ring Around
The Rosy,
Not Another Ghosty

Chapter 1

Spring had finally arrived. It took its time getting here and by mid-April I was certain that it would never come, but here it is, warm and glorious with lots of flowers blooming in everyone's freshly mulched flowerbeds. I was so glad that it was May, and classes would be ending soon. I had finals left, but wasn't too worried about that. At least I no longer needed my winter coat, and on most days I was able to ditch my jacket.

To celebrate the arrival of spring, and Jackie's birthday, Greg and I decided to take her out. The circus had arrived in town: a traveling circus that had been making the circuit all over New England for the past month and Greg had managed to get three tickets. I had reminded him that it was her birthday—she was turning the dreaded 29, that last mark before 30—and I wanted to make it something special. So, instead of the usual outing at a nice restaurant, Greg came home with some tickets for the much talked about circus. The entire town could not stop talking about it.

I couldn't wait, and I knew Jackie would be excited. She like watching the performances and all of the tricks that they did, not to mention the animals.

"Are you ready?" I asked her, tucking my keys into my jeans pocket.

"Almost," came Jackie's voice. She marched out of the bathroom, finishing her mascara and touching up her lip gloss before stopping. "Look at you!"

"What?" I said, taking a quick glance in the hallway mirror at my muscle tank top and jeans. I didn't see a problem with the way I was dressed, but compared to Jackie's skinny jeans, with a jeweled belt, shimmering purple top, and beret hat, with a green band around it, I looked like I had crawled out of a junkyard.

"I'm surprised you're able to keep that man of yours around."

"I think it's because he cares about more than just the way I look."

In response, Jackie seized my arm and yanked me into my room where she threw open my closet, almost gasping at what she saw. "Geez, Mel, you need to update your wardrobe."

I looked at the boot cut jeans, t-shirts, tank tops, my one winter coat, and the jade jacket that Jackie had bought for me when we first moved to Vermont, not sure what was wrong with it. "They're the same clothes I always wear."

Jackie reached in and pulled out a black, sports tank with a semi-faded silver heart on it. "I remember when you wore this in high school. You were 16!"

"Yeah, but it still fits and it's functional," I replied.

"That was 13 years ago," said Jackie, tossing the tank top into the wastebasket. "Tomorrow, you're going shopping for an updated look."

I grimaced. I hated shopping. It just wasn't one of my favorite activities, but Jackie was right, I needed to replace the outdated clothes in my closet.

"Come on," said Jackie, dragging me into her room and yanking the door to her closet open, regaling me with ruffled blouses, slacks, yoga pants, trouser jeans, sleeveless shirts that could be worn for both casual and formal wear, and a whole trove of shoes. She positioned me by the closet's doorframe and reached in, pulling out shirt after shirt and holding each one up to me, discerning if it was fit for me to wear. Within two minutes, she had gone through half her closet before pulling out a burnt orange, satin top with a high collar and no sleeves.

"Perfect!" said Jackie, shoving it into my hands.

I changed, knowing that I would never get out of it, and once I had, she pushed me into the bathroom.

"Now for some makeup."

"I'm already wearing foundation and eye shadow," I said.

Jackie pushed her face into mine, until there was only two inches between us, scrutinizing my makeup. "Well, you are wearing some, but you need something more to make you stand out."

I thought the colorful top she had me put on would make me stand out enough.

Before I knew it, Jackie had put on some blush, eyeliner, mascara, and touched up my eye shadow. She turned me until I faced the mirror. After all the years I had known her, I still could not believe how she managed to put makeup on me without it ever looking as though I wore any. I had to admit that I looked good.

"Now, you look like a woman getting ready to hit 30 in a few months," said Jackie.

"So do you," I teased.

"Nope!" said Jackie. "That's not for an official 12 months."

I grinned, remembering how when we were teenagers we both thought that 30 was old.

"Hey, didn't Mr. Stilton ask you to pick some stuff up for him before you go back to work?" asked Jackie.

"Yes, but the warehouse won't be open until tomorrow morning. I'll pick them up then before heading into work."

"Why'd he ask you to get them anyway?"

"No idea," I replied. "He might have been too lazy to get them himself." I glanced at my watch. "Greg is probably wondering where we are."

As though to prove my point, a knock sounded at the door. I rushed out of the bathroom and answered it.

"You girls ready?" asked Greg. "There's the birthday girl," he said when Jackie appeared.

He held out his arms for both of us to each take one and I found myself glad to have found a fiancé who didn't mind taking my best friend out for her birthday bash; though, I think he had been looking forward to the circus as well, but didn't want to admit it.

"Where's Tiny?" Greg asked.

"He said he would meet us later tonight," I replied. "Something about clowns scaring him."

Chapter 2

When we arrived at the circus, it was clear that we were not the only ones who wanted to see the show and enjoy the nicer weather. Greg moved the car at a snail's pace as he steered around meandering crowds of parents pushing strollers and tugging toddlers along. The sand-filled, makeshift parking lot crunched under the tires with each slow rotation they made as Greg headed for a space just big enough and pulled in.

We each got out of the car and joined the lines going into the giant tent where the main attraction was. Jackie jumped up and down with excitement. I didn't remember her ever loving the circus before, but then, we had never been to one. Flirty and whimsical music played in the background as we entered the opening of the tent, plunging into darkness, compared to walking in the bright sunshine.

"We're over here," said Greg, glancing at the ticket in his hand and leading us up the stands towards the back row.

We sat on the metal bleachers, which reminded me of my high school days, and looked down at the ring below with the dancing flags that moved from the breeze that spilled through the entranceway, and the bright shimmers that bobbed up and down. The stands wobbled as more people, led by a woman who was very out of shape, climbed them, proving to be unsteady on their feet, and sat behind us with the woman gasping from the exertion.

"Hey, Mel! Jackie!" shouted a familiar voice, garnering a groan from Jackie as what looked like a bright, neon orange, pink, and green sign carrying a bag of popcorn ran up to us, climbing over the seats, instead of using the allotted steps.

"You two never told me that you were planning on coming here today."

"Probably because we didn't want you here," mumbled Jackie and I nudged her with my elbow, reminding her to be nice.

"Hi, Tammy," I said with a fake smile. "We… uh… were just having a small—private—celebration of Jackie's birthday."

"Oh, happy birthday!" shrieked Tammy, leaping over the seat in front of me and smacking into Jackie as she tried to give her a giant hug while fluffy kernels of popcorn flew all over the place. "I didn't know it was your birthday!"

More popcorn spilled from the bag in her hand, landing near Jackie's feet, who stood with her arms crossed as her mouth formed a thin, tight line.

"How old are you?" asked Tammy.

"Aren't those your friends down there?" said Jackie in a curt tone.

"Oh, just my family." Tammy waved at a pair of bright purple jumpsuits with pastel red dots all over them. Guess now we all knew where she got her fashion sense from.

"Shouldn't you be sitting with them?" said Jackie, her voice getting a dangerous edge to it; one that I had known her to use only twice in our lifetime.

"Oh, don't worry about them," said Tammy, giving an exuberant wave and knocking the soda out of the hands of the person standing in the row above us. Brown, bubbly and sticky liquid washed all over Jackie's leopard printed flats. She raised her fist to punch Tammy, but I seized it before she was able to follow through on her plans.

"Perhaps, we should sit down," I said. "Calm down," I whispered in Jackie's ear when Tammy's back was turned.

She jerked her hand from my grasp and plopped on the metal seat with a huff. Tammy, remaining oblivious to the fact that she had just escaped receiving a black eye, sat next to Jackie, shoving a handful of popcorn into her mouth before offering some to Jackie who refused.

A man in a red suit, with gold coattails flapping behind him walked into the ring, waving a switch around in a gesture meant to get everyone's attention.

"Ladies and gentlemen," said the ringleader, speaking into the microphone. "Welcome!"

Claps and cheers rang out and I nudged Jackie, reminding her that we were here for the circus, not to
watch Tammy munch on popcorn.

"Be prepared to be amazed," continued the ringleader, "as we show you marvels of the exploits that can be
achieved by humans!"

More cheers roared around us as the ringleader
turned a circle with his arms outstretched.

"Give it up for Serina and her horse!"

The ringleader stepped aside as a woman dressed in
golden leotards and a purple tutu rode out on a white
horse covered in sequins. The horse's hooves clomped on
the sand, sending a few poofs of dust into the already
dusty air as it galloped in a circle amidst more cheers. The
rider rose up and stood on the saddle of the horse as it
galloped, before jumping on a trampoline that had been
brought into the middle of the ring. She bounced up and
down, doing flips and leaps while the horse continued to
run in a circle around her. As the crowd watched with
bated breath—even Jackie was enthralled, despite having
been irritated earlier—as the woman did a back flip and
landed in the saddle of the horse where she bowed and
waved her arms, accepting the applause that filled the
area before riding out of the ring.

"Ladies and gentlemen, give it up for Serina!" shouted the ringleader and more claps and cheers rang out.

"That was awesome!" screamed Tammy, jumping up
and down; her movements rocked the bleachers while
popcorn flew from the squished bag in her hands.

"It is time for death defying leaps," continued the

ringleader, "fiery infernos, and the acrobatic skill of the Jumping Durangos!"

I stood up to get a better look as six people dressed in green outfits that twinkled and reflected the ceiling lights ran into the ring, doing a combination of cartwheels, flips, jumps, and somersaults, while waving and smiling at the crowd. One, knocked over a stand, sending the lit torch that is held flying across the ring before it landed in the sand and went out. People laughed, thinking it was part of the act, but I had my doubts as she stood there, staring at the fallen stand with a slender hand over her mouth. One of the other performers must have called to her because she turned—her curly ponytail swinging from side to side—and ran to the others, doing her best to blend in with the stunts they performed.

We all watched in awe as the biggest of the bunch lit a hoop on fire, stepped back, ran, and jumped through it, doing a forward somersault as he landed before ending with a back flip. The tent erupted in roars of cheers and praise. The man looked back at the female performer I had noticed earlier. She stared at the hoop before racing to it, but just as she was about to jump through, she tripped and fell through the hoop, while her left foot slammed into the pole that supported it, knocking it over, and sending it crashing around her. The other acrobats rushed to her, helping her up and putting out the flames. Again the crowd believed that it had been a part of the act and applauded with enthusiasm, yelling for more. The poor woman smiled, but I could tell that she was embarrassed.

"She's good with that clumsy act of hers," whispered Jackie in my ear.

"Yeah," I said, allowing the word to drag out as I watched her stumble a little and shake her head, still unsure if her mishaps were an act or not. No one noticed as the woman reached out to grab hold of something before she fell over. "I think there might be something wrong with her."

No one heard me over the crowd.

"OOOOO," said the people around me as one of the performers stuck a rope in her mouth and allowed herself to be pulled into the air.

She twirled in a circle with her feet arced in a way where she looked like a hook. Once she had reached the desired height, she did a sort of dance in the air, swaying from side to side in fluid movements, reminding me of the way strands of a spider's web float in a breeze. She let go. The crowd gasped as the woman dropped before being caught by a man on a swing as he rushed past and both landed on a platform, bowing and waving amongst the applause.

I watched as the woman clutched her throat. "I don't think she can breathe!" I yelled, shaking Greg's shoulder and pointing the poor woman out to him.

The other acrobats on the ground formed a circle, preparing for their next routine when they stopped. Hushed silence fell over everyone in the bleachers as they waited with bated breath for the next performance, but a roar met their expectations instead. Before anyone had time to react, a tiger ran out into the ring. The acrobats darted away in different directions, but the woman I was concerned about froze. We watched in horror as she backed away into a corner, as the tiger drew nearer, trapped. In a heartbeat, the animal was upon her, clawing at her before being ripped away by a man with a whip and leash. He called the tiger by name and the animal stopped, flopping on the ground and rolling over onto its back as though it had been playing a game. The man with the leash, hooked it to the tiger's collar and led it away with ease, while the tent erupted in murmurs and whispers about what had happened, but my eyes stayed focused on the poor, unmoving girl.

The ringleader rushed to the microphone. "Ladies and gentlemen I need you to remain in your seats. We've had an incident."

Some people stood up and walked out of the tent while others gathered around the woman on the ground.

"Please remain in your seats!" yelled the ringleader in the microphone, but no one listened to him.

I jumped from my seat and ran down the bleachers, stepping on the metal rows with a loud bang as I rushed to the ring, determined to get a look at the woman's body before the gathering crowd had a chance to mess it up.

"Mel!" shouted Greg as he chased after me.

Jackie followed muttering, "Not again!"

I glanced back just in time to see Tammy jump up and come after us with an exuberant look on her face as she tossed aside her crumpled popcorn bag. I raced down to the ring, passing a group of panicked people as they darted in front of me, desperate to get out of the tent.

Once I reached the bottom row, I jumped off, landing on a soft mound of dirt, and managing to not lose my balance, as I ran to the ring and the woman.

"Mel!"

Greg's voice followed after me as I shoved my way through the mass of bodies before me while they tried to satisfy their curiosity and get a good look at the unfortunate woman.

"Hey!" shouted one as I pushed him to the side, forcing him to his knees.

While the ringleader remained busy, and others pulled out their phones to call the police and take pictures, I knelt by the woman's body. Her eyes still held that frightened look. I closed them. There wasn't much to see beyond her torn clothing and heavy makeup, but beneath one of the ripped sleeves was a bit of discoloration—a brownish and blue mark around where the tiger's claw had gotten her.

"Mel"—Greg knelt beside me—"what are..."

I pointed at the discoloration on the skin around the claw mark and his brows scrunched together as his thoughts joined mine: this was odd. He pulled out his phone a snapped a picture just as a few of the circus performers had arrived and forced us to leave.

"Get away from there!" one of them snapped at me as he hauled me to my feet before Greg shoved him away.

"We're going," he said to the man, his voice firm.

We found Jackie and dragged her with us as we left the tent, with Tammy trailing behind, chatting about how happy she was to have another mystery to solve. I wondered if it had occurred to her that someone had just died.

We got outside just as the first police car pulled up,

with a four door sedan right behind it, which I recognized as Detective Shorts' car. I had no idea how I was going to explain this, nor did I have a chance to think of something since he must have spotted me with Greg and Jackie and parked right in front of us.

"I had a feeling you would be here," he said as he got out of the car and closed the door while Tammy hopped from foot to foot in excitement.

"Before you start to…" I began, but he cut me off with a wave of his hand.

"So, tell me what happened."

"One of the acrobats got murdered!" shrieked Tammy, jumping up and down behind me, unable to contain her enthusiasm at having a second chance to help solve a mystery. A couple years ago, during the Christmas parade, I had witnessed a woman get murdered and Tammy had decided to join me in discovering who had done it, since at the time Jackie and I were having a disagreement about her choice of a boyfriend. Though, it didn't help that her boyfriend had actually been the one who committed the murder. Anyway, ever since, Tammy has been badgering me to let her help in unraveling another murder mystery, with me doing my best to ignore her. I guess I won't be able to do that this time.

Detective Shorts raised an eyebrow at Tammy's outburst. "You are happy that someone has died?" he asked her with a reprimanding note in his voice, the sort a parent uses when correcting their child.

"No," replied Tammy, shrinking under his gaze, trying to hide behind me.

"Your name?"

"Tammy! I'm their friend."

"That's debatable," murmured Jackie under her breath, but by the way Detective Shorts glanced in her direction, I knew he had heard her.

"Tell me, in your own words, what happened."

"Well…" I started to say, but Tammy interrupted me.

"She was attacked and mauled by a vicious tiger. It stalked her and hunted her down, hoping to get a piece of fresh meat to satisfy its carnivorous taste buds." She slouched a bit, using animated movements to act out her story while the rest of us stared at her with confused looks on our faces.

"Wow," said Jackie in a condescending tone. "You should write fiction."

I looked at her, trying to remind her to be nice, but she just folded her arms and stepped back. I knew she was disappointed about how her birthday celebration had turned out, and she and Tammy didn't get along. Jackie had always found Tammy's personality to be about as welcomed as a cockroach on the wall. Not that I blamed her; Tammy took a little getting used to and tended to get on everybody's nerves.

"That isn't really what happened," said Greg.

"Yes, it is," protested Tammy and Jackie snorted in response. "Well… I might have embellished a few things."

"Try the entire story," said Jackie.

We stopped talking when Detective Shorts tapped his pen on the small notepad within his hand in irritation. "Does one of you want to tell me exactly what happened?"

"We came here to celebrate Jackie's birthday—"

"Happy birthday!" shrieked Tammy.

"—and the acrobatic act had just begun when the tiger got out," I finished.

"And what happened next?" asked Detective Shorts.

"Most everyone panicked," replied Greg, "but the woman who was attacked froze. Before we knew it, she was on the ground and the tiger was on top of her."

"And it growled and..." Tammy stopped speaking when she noticed Detective Shorts' warning look.

"That was when the trainer came out and got the tiger," said Jackie. "I'm not sure wat he said to it, but it just rolled over and purred."

"And after that?" asked the detective.

"After that," replied Greg, "some gathered around the woman on the ground while others ran out of the tent."

"And where were you?" Detective Shorts pointed at me. He knew me too well.

"I was in the bleachers."

He gave me his evil eye.

"I might have run down and checked on the woman."

"Excuse me," said a woman, shoving her way through, "how much longer must I stay here? I have things to do."

"Ma'am, I need you to be patient. One of my officers will take a statement and then you may leave."

She walked off in a huff, angered at having to stay longer.

"You four can go," said Detective Shorts to us. "And Miss Summers, I don't... Oh, what the hell—you're going to get involved anyway." He shoved his notepad back into his breast pocket and walked off.

"So, what now?" asked Jackie.

"I think…" I began, but once again Tammy cut me off.

"We catch a murderer! Who do you think did it?" She stared at me with sand dollar-sized eyes, anticipating my response.

"Greg, do you have a rope in your car?" asked Jackie.

"I might," he replied, pulling out his keys, but I shoved his arm down.

"Stop it you two," I hissed at them. I looked around at all of the people meandering about, their patience running thin as they waited for the police to tell them they could leave. Two people from the Medical Examiner's office came out of the tent, rolling a gurney with a body bag on it, no doubt with the poor woman's body inside. "We need to find somewhere to hide while we wait for this place to clear out."

A sharp whistle pierced my ears, forcing me to turn around and I found Tammy poking her head out of a barrel, motioning for us to come over.

"Come on," I said, running over to Tammy. It turned out that she had found about eight barrels, which were either empty or had some hay within them, stashed behind the tent and next to a wagon.

"I knew you wouldn't want to let them solve this," whispered Tammy, indicating the police.

I hated to admit it, but Tammy had a good idea about hiding in the barrels until everyone left. I glanced at Jackie and Greg.

"You know, this is not how I had wanted to celebrate my birthday," she said to me, "but I'm just as curious as you, so scoot over." She lifted the top off one of the barrels, pulled the hay out, stuffing it under the wagon, and crawled inside, placing the lid back in place so that nothing looked out of the ordinary.

"After you," said Greg, holding the lid of a barrel open for me.

"You're the best." I kissed him and crawled inside.

"Now, nobody make a sound," said Tammy, once we were all in our respective barrels. I don't know if she could have said it any louder.

"Then, shut up!" hissed Jackie.

After a half hour passed, I started to reconsider the whole hiding in a barrel thing. When an hour went by, I wished that Tammy had found a better spot. Despite the fact that it was only 65 degrees outside, inside the barrel I was in it felt as though the temperature had reached 100 as the sides reflected my body heat, which caused more sweat to stream down my face and back, not to mention that my legs had cramped and I wished that I could just stretch them.

A car door slammed.

"Are they leaving now?" asked Jackie.

I lifted the lid to my barrel and peeked out. Just about everyone had gone and only a few officers remained. I watched as the last of them got in their cars and left. Detective Shorts opened the door to his sedan and looked in my direction, giving me that uneasy feeling that he knew where I was and what I was up to, before crawling in the driver's seat and speeding away. Relieved, I jumped up, tossing the barrel lid aside, which soon turned out to be a bad idea as my legs screamed at me, having forgotten how to move after having been in a fetal position for the last hour.

Three more barrel lids thumped on the ground as Jackie, Greg, and Tammy crawled out, groaning when they forced their stiff legs and arms to bend and move. I hurried to the tent entrance with the others right behind me, running past a couple more barrels. One of them toppled over, spilling its contents. I didn't remember touching it.

"Geez, Mel, be careful," said Jackie.

Not wanting to say anything—I mean, I could have knocked it over in my eagerness to get inside—I ran through the tent flaps and stopped, taking a quick look around. It seemed to be empty. "She was over there," I said and hurried to the ring.

"What are we looking for?" asked Jackie.

"Not sure," I said, "but doesn't the entire thing seem odd? Animals don't just attack people. Greg, will you show her the picture?"

Greg pulled out his phone and showed the picture of the claw mark on the woman to Jackie.

"What's that discoloration there?" asked Jackie.

"Not sure," said Greg, "but that is what has us curious."

Tammy snatched Greg's hand with the phone to get a good look at it. "That looks nasty!"

Jackie opened her mouth to say something, but closed it, which I thought was more prudent of her.

The four of us split up and we each took a separate corner of the ring, scouring the ground, looking for anything out of the ordinary. I didn't expect to find anything, but one thing I learned after I started getting involved in murder cases was that the smallest detail can be vital, and usually goes unnoticed by most; but I didn't seem to be finding anything, which sometimes happened. Footprints lay everywhere and the sand had been kicked up into tiny drifts, but nothing stood out of the ordinary.

I turned and spotted a small brown spot on the light-colored sand. A few inches away was another. I circled on my feet and noticed several more brown splotches on the sand, some of them had faded, but others were quite dark. I followed them, marking how they formed a patterns until it hit me: the marks fell right where a tiger's paws would when it ran and they formed a line stretching to another area of the tent. I started to head over there when…

"Tammy! What the heck are you doing?" screamed Jackie, looking at the ceiling.

An uneasy feeling washed over me as I craned my neck and looked upward. On the wire above, no doubt the high wire used by some of the performers, stood Tammy with a pole in her arms, inching her way across. There was one thing missing: the safety net. It had been put away. "Tammy, what are you doing?" I shouted upward.

Tammy continued to balance on the wire, placing one foot in front of the other. "I always wanted to do the high wire," she said, her voice spilling with enthusiasm, unconcerned about the danger she was in if she lost her balance and fell.

As I watched her, I had to admit that she was good, and possessed better balance and skill than me when it came to walking on a wire. I searched for the net and notice a hand crank attached to a mechanism that looked as though it had the net rolled up on it.

"Greg, help me with this." I ran for the crank and reached up to pull on it, but Greg pushed me aside and heaved. It squeaked with each turn he gave it as the netting stretched across underneath Tammy.

"Hey," said Tammy, unaware that she was giving us each a heart attack, "look what I can do." She raised the pole in front of her, leaned forward, and balanced on her left foot. "If I put my arm out like this, it looks as though I'm flying!"

A part of me wanted to climb up there and push her off that rope for her stupidity. Karma must have felt the same as that tiny part of me did because, at that moment, Tammy's balance faltered and she fell to the right, dropping the pole, which crashed to the ground with a soft thud. I gritted my teeth and bit my tongue from anxiety, but Greg had managed to get the net stretched out in time and Tammy sank into it, before being flung upward into the air and landing in the net a second time where she bounced around for a little bit before stopping.

"That was so much fun!" said Tammy, her face bursting with excitement.

I ran past the hoops to join Greg and Jackie who had already reached the net. Within seconds of me passing them, they fell over, crashing into the ground and making so much noise, I was certain that someone would hear us. Both Jackie and Greg gave me questioning looks before turning back to Tammy to help her off the net.

"Were you born with sawdust for brains?" demanded Jackie of her.

"You should try it," said Tammy. "That will get your heart pumping in the morning."

"Do you have any idea how stupid that was?" Jackie continued. "What do you think would have happened if we hadn't gotten that net put in place before you fell?"

"Didn't really think about that," said Tammy, looking at her shoes, which had been bedazzled at some point, though some of the sparkling buttons had fallen off, revealing gray leather beneath.

Jackie rolled her eyes, giving Tammy a "no kidding" look.

"What is going on in here?" demanded an irate voice.

Yep, someone had heard us. It was the ringleader.

"Well?" he stopped in front of us with his bushy eyebrows squished together and his hands on his hips.

None of us said anything. What could we say?

"I want an explanation now."

I decided that we had to say something. "We were just—"

"Looking for the real murderer!" Once again, Tammy interrupted me and I found myself sharing Jackie's desire to strangle her, especially after that high wire fiasco.

"Excuse me?" said the ringleader.

"It's nothing," said Greg, shoving Tammy behind him before she could say another word. "We were just leaving."

"Right you are. Follow me. Now."

We trailed after him, knowing that there was little else to do, walking past some poles, similar to what Tammy had used while walking on the wire, that leaned against the wall, but just as I neared them, they tipped over, garnering more quizzical looks from Jackie and Greg. Tammy remained oblivious to all of it as she stared at the high wire, probably hoping to climb up there again. I noticed the ringleader staring at me as well, though he had a strange look on his face, one that conveyed that I reminded him of someone. He led us outside into the sun, which hurt my eyes after being in the dark tent for the last 20 minutes, saying, "Detective!"

Oh no. Detective Shorts walked up and the irritated look on his face told me that he was not surprised to see us.

"Hey," said Tammy, pointing at him, "I thought you had left. That's why we went in there in the first place. Can't be snooping around when you—"

Jackie seized Tammy and placed a hand over her mouth, trying to get her to stop talking, but she continued speak despite the fact that her words sounded muffled. "Pay no attention to her," smiled Jackie. "She's still suffering from that adrenaline rush after her little misadventure."

"I want you to arrest these four for trespassing," said the ringleader.

"It won't do much good," said Detective Shorts under his breath.

"What?" asked the ringleader.

Detective Shorts cleared his throat. "Are you sure? These sorts of cases get tied up in the courts and can drag out, and something tells me you don't want to be in town too long."

"Just get them out of here."

"I'm just wondering," I said, Tammy's boldness must

have rubbed off on me, "why is it you did nothing when that woman was attacked?"

"What are you talking about?"

"You just stood there," I said to the ringleader. "You didn't seem that concerned at all that the tiger had pinned her to the ground."

"How dare you! I don't have to answer you."

Detective Shorts closed the distance between them. "No, but she brings up a valid point and I am curious. I must ask you to answer the question Mr.…."

"Al," spat the ringleader.

The two men glared at one another for a minute before Al broke the silence.

"It's not that I wasn't concerned about her, or didn't try to help. It's true that I did not react the way everyone else did, but I… I don't feel emotions, especially fear, the way most do. My whole life I have had a sort of emotional detachment. I don't feel fear, joy, or sadness, the way most do. That may be why it appeared that I didn't react."

A firm line formed on the detective's face. I don't know if he believed Al or not, but for the moment, he was satisfied and let the matter drop. "Let's go, you four," he said to us as Al went back inside the tent.

"I thought you had left," I said to him.

"I had a feeling that you would be up to something, so I stuck around, letting you believe that I had gone."

I should have known. After a few years of running into me whenever a body turned up, I shouldn't be surprised that Detective Shorts had guessed that I would remain to conduct my own investigation.

"I want you four to go home."

"Yes, sir," I said.

"I mean it."

I nodded in response. We all piled into Greg's car, and since the people who had accompanied Tammy to the circus had already left, we had no choice but to take her home as well.

"That was so much fun," Tammy said as she crawled into the back seat with Jackie. "Oh, and it's your birthday! We must go out and celebrate."

Jackie's eyes widened. "I am so tired," she said, faking a yawn, "I think I should just go home and rest."

"Maybe next time," Tammy replied as she turned to stare out the window with a huge smile on her face.

Chapter 3

We dropped Tammy off at her house and left her standing on the sidewalk waving like a hyper-spasdic bird at us. Afterward, we just went home. We were all beat and Greg had an early shift the next morning so we called it day.

"You get some sleep," I told Greg as we stood in front of his door and kissed him.

"And you stay out of trouble."

"Always do," I replied with a mischievous smile, because we all knew that I had a propensity to find trouble, or trouble tended to find me. "See you in the morning."

"You two are so old-fashioned," commented Jackie as we walked into our apartment.

"What do you mean?"

"Oh, the kissing at the doorway. The fact that you two are engaged and haven't moved in together."

"Just because we are engaged doesn't mean we have to live together. Time enough for that after the 'I dos'. Plus, we still have a lease on this place and I'm not going to leave you stuck with paying my share of the rent. And then there is Aunt Ethel."

Jackie dropped the pillow from the couch that she had been fiddling with, jerked around and snatched me by the shoulders, shaking me. "Please tell me she is not stopping by for another visit! Don't mess with me, Mel. Please tell she isn't coming!"

I almost laughed at the panicked look on Jackie's face, except that I shared her sentiments about my Aunt Ethel visiting us again. "No... not right now anyway."

"What do you mean, not right now?"

"Well..." I began, "I received a letter from her last week."

"And?"

"And she mentioned something about being lonely, wanting more excitement, and how she was thinking of putting her house up for sale."

"And where, might I ask, is she planning to move to?" Jackie crossed her arms and I think she already guessed the answer.

"Here," I replied.

"That's it!" said Jackie. "I am dead bolting that door. In fact, I'm putting two deadbolts on it. Wait. So is that why you and Greg haven't moved in together?"

"Partly. When we do, we want it to be a place that we picked out together. Start new and fresh. But I have a feeling that if I were to move in with him now, Aunt Ethel might get the idea to—"

"No! No! And no! I am not living with your Aunt Ethel. You and Greg need to pick out this beautiful house with a separate apartment to it that I can live in. I don't make much noise and I'll pay double the rent. Please! If you leave me alone I know she's going to move in with me."

"Which is why I'm still here. Besides, both Greg and I want to graduate from college first before we get married so you have nothing to worry about."

Jackie cocked her head to the side, her hair falling in silky waves as she gave me a doubtful expression. She knew my aunt too well.

"Oh, come on. My aunt isn't that bad. She's just…"

"Psychotic."

I gave Jackie a reproachful glare. "Eccentric."

"That's putting it mildly."

I chuckled at Jackie's antics, but she had a point: my aunt could be a handful—two handfuls. A huge part of me hoped that she would get the idea of moving to Vermont out of her head, but knowing my aunt, she had already bought a place.

I walked to the refrigerator in the kitchen to get a bottle of tea and when I passed the table, the vase on it flew off, smashing into the linoleum floor and shattered while the pieces scattered in a puddle of water and the flowers formed a circle around it. I stared at the broken vase. I hadn't touched it. I knew I hadn't touched it, so how did it just crash to the floor like that?

Jackie stepped up beside me. "You know, you've become quite the klutz since we left the circus."

I ignored her and yanked the fridge open, snatching a bottle of tea in there. "I think I'm going to go to bed," I said, popping the top off the bottle and taking a long drink.

"I didn't mean it as an insult."

"It's not that. It's just… It's been a long day."

"Night then."

That night I lay in bed, unable to sleep. Instead all I did was toss and turn and every time my eyes started to droop, something would make me pop awake again. Why couldn't I sleep? I knew why. I kept thinking about the circus and that poor woman. It didn't make sense, her dying like that; but then what did I know about tiger attacks? Though, I still refused to believe that the reason for Al's lack of response was just because he doesn't experience emotions like most normal people.

My mind wrestled with the day's events. After an hour of debating with myself about what did or could have happened, I decided that, in the end there was nothing to be done. By all accounts, it looked like the poor woman had died because of the tiger's attack. I just wish I knew why it had charged her in the first place. And how did it get out of its cage?

A thunderous crash echoed in the hallway just outside my bedroom. What in the world was going on? I knew it wasn't me this time. I shoved the blankets off me and hurried to my door, pushing it open as I peered out into the dark hallway. No one there. The hair on the back of my neck stood up as an uneasy feeling that Jackie and I were not alone in the apartment washed over me. I knelt by the fallen picture frame, being careful and avoiding the broken glass, just as Jackie opened the door to her room and stepped out.

"Mel, what's going on?"

"Not sure."

"Did you knock that off the wall?" she asked, noticing the picture frame for the first time.

"It wasn't me."

"But there is no one else in here."

I didn't say anything.

"There is no one else here, right?"

Just then, Jackie's porcelain hummingbird figurine fell from the shelf it was on in the living room, followed by a disembodied "Oops". I cringed when I heard the tinkle of the broken pieces skip across the floor. It was one of her favorite decorative items and I didn't need to see her face to know that her brow had furrowed and her nose had pinched itself in anger. I took a step towards the living room, but Jackie shoved her hand out, stopping me, and forced her way past as she marched into the room.

"AHHHHH!" she screamed and I rushed to her, turning on a light.

Yep. Her porcelain hummingbird figurine had been knocked off its shelf and shattered on the floor.

"My great-grandmother had given that to me!" Jackie wailed.

It was true. Her great-grandmother's grandmother had made that figurine by hand when her ancestors still lived in Korea before her great-grandparents had immigrated to the United States. It was a family heirloom that had been passed down to Jackie and was one of her most prized possessions.

I braced myself for the firestorm I knew would happen, not that I would blame her; if I had a family heirloom like that, I know how I would react.

A thud sounded and the plant hanging in the far corner of the room fell from its hook, landing on its side with water spilling everywhere on the once pristine white carpet. A few seconds later, the TV toppled over, to which both Jackie and I cringed, fearing that it would break.

"I'm sorry," came a faint whisper and I knew what was going on.

Jackie turned her head towards me, her eyes in slits as her lips formed a thin line on her mouth. "Please tell me that something didn't follow you home."

I shrugged my shoulders, about to respond when—
CRASH!

The replica of a grandfather clock that sat near the TV had fallen over, smashing into the mirror that hung on the wall next to it, sending shards of glass in every direction.

"Seven years' bad luck," mumbled Jackie with her arms crossed.

"Oh, dear," came the same disembodied voice.

I had to do something before even more of a mess was made. "Stop!" I yelled. "We know you are here, whoever you are, so, please, just show yourself."

"I'm not sure how," the voice whispered.

Jackie released an exasperated sigh.

"Uh... think solid," I said, not sure what to tell her, much less how Rachel always managed to be visible when she needed to be.

A slender arm, wrapped in glittery, sheer green material appeared.

"Okay, that's good," I said, trying to encourage her. "A little bit more."

A head appeared, but it looked down at the arm and shrieked before vanishing.

Doing my best to remain patient, since dying can me a traumatic experience, I kept my voice calm as I spoke. "You were doing great. Just try to make the rest of you solid."

A figure appeared, though faint, flickering in and out before it solidified and resembled a real live person. I almost gasped when I realized who it was: the woman that had been attacked by the tiger. I shouldn't have been surprised, but a part of me couldn't believe that she was here, and so soon.

"What can I do for you?" I asked, already guessing the answer.

Jackie just stared at the ghost, and I realized that she had managed to make herself visible for both of us; either that, or didn't know that she could pick and choose who saw her.

"I've been following you around and realized that you seem to be able to sense that I was here, or that is the feeling I got."

I found myself thanking Rachel for that.

"So, I've been following you all day to see if my suspicions were correct." She stepped forward and knocked over a lamp that would had fallen on the floor if Jackie hadn't leapt over the couch and caught it.

Well, that explains why everywhere I went today, chaos followed. "I'm not sure how I can help," I said. "The police are certain that your death was a tragic accident."

"Oh no," said the ghost, "I'm aware that it was, but I just wanted to know if you could get a message to my parents for me."

"Oh," I replied, hoping that this visit would be a quick one, "sure."

"It might help if we knew your name," said Jackie, who had gotten used to the fact that ghosts sometimes show up, some of whom have no problems interacting with both of us and others who tended to be more shy. This ghost seemed to be one of the shier ones as Jackie's curt voice caused her to fade some.

"No, don't go," I said, moving towards her. "It's late and that was Jackie's figurine that broke. It was a family heirloom."

The ghost solidified again, shuffling her feet. "I'm very sorry about that," she said. "I'm just such a klutz sometimes."

She waved her hands and a book fell off the bookcase she stood in front of. Muttering apologies to us, she picked up the book, fumbling with it as it slipped between her ethereal fingers before knocking the entire bookcase over in her efforts to hold onto the dancing paperback. The bookcase slammed into the back of the chair with books flying off the shelves, littering the carpet. I gritted my teeth, hoping that the noise hadn't woken our downstairs neighbors.

"Oh dear," said the ghost.

She had reached down to clean up when Jackie stopped her. "Why don't I do that and you give Mel the information she needs to contact your family."

The ghost agreed.

I walked over to the kitchen and sat at the table while Jackie grabbed the vacuum cleaner to sweep up the broken glass. "Can you give me your name?" I asked the ghost.

She faced me, realizing that in all the commotion, she had never told me her name. "Cheryl."

"What would you like me to say to your parents?"

Cheryl wrung her hands together in nervousness. "It's complicated."

"How so?"

"I'm originally from Vancouver."

I waited for her to continue, wondering why she suddenly seemed nervous about calling her family.

She pulled a chair out to sit down, but ended up knocking it over instead, which garnered an eye roll from Jackie. "My parents are well to do. They were both born into it and their marriage was arranged by their parents to ensure that the wealth stayed within the family and when I became of legal age to marry, they decided to arrange my wedding as well."

"Seems old-fashioned," commented Jackie.

"They just thought that it all should stay within the family. It isn't a new idea and a lot of families still participate in such practices."

"Well, I guess if you are of that stock..."Jackie continued.

"Not necessarily," I interrupted her. "Remember the

Wilsons downstairs? They had a son who decided to get engaged, but they were livid at who he had chosen as his fiancé. And they have about as much money as we do."

Jackie thought about that a moment and remembered that a month ago Jason Wilson had eloped with his girlfriend, despite his parents' protests. "I guess no matter where you come from, some people want to control their children's lives."

I nodded and turned back to Cheryl. "So, what did you do?"

"I detested the man they had chosen for me. He came from money of course and was a successful businessman, but I didn't love him and I didn't want to get married. Not right then, anyway."

"Was he a jerk?" I asked.

Cheryl grimaced. "No. He was actually quite nice and willing to put up with my clumsiness, but I wasn't ready for marriage and felt like my life had been all planned out for me. So, I ran away. The circus, the same one you were at today, had been in Vancouver when I left home. I snuck into one of the performer's tents. It wasn't long before I was discovered."

I could guess why, as Cheryl swung her arm and knocked a forgotten cup to the floor.

"It was the acrobats' tent," continued Cheryl. "Roz, she was the oldest one there and had seniority, listened to my story and talked the owner into letting me stay."

"You joined their act?"

"Yeah. Some of the others didn't like the fact that I was there due to my tendency of breaking things. I was born a klutz. I swear I was. Ever since I can remember, I have been knocking things over without meaning to and whenever I try to be careful, more things get broken."

"It's okay," I reassured her, even though I was a bit aggravated by the mess in the next room. "What did your parents do?"

"I stayed with the circus, traveling across the country, and when we reached Phoenix, I sent a postcard home, informing my parents of what I had done and where I was."

"What happened next?"

"My father posted an ad in the paper, stating that he had disinherited me."

"Seems a bit harsh," said Jackie.

"Oh, he was angry and I'm certain that my actions did hurt him and my mother, not to mention Trevor, the man they had chosen as my future husband. I had tried calling them a few times, but my father always hung up on me. After that, I just remained with Roz and the circus. I like it and she had figured out how to incorporate my clumsiness into the act. I just wish that the tiger's cage and been more secure."

A gloomy look crossed her face as she thought about the reality of her death and I felt sorry for her.

"I need to at least let my parents know that I'm not mad at them for what they did. I'd been thinking about it a lot and had even considered going back for a visit and would have if…"

I walked over to my purse and pulled my phone out. Though it was almost midnight here, it would be nine at night in Washington state, due to the three-hour time difference. "What is their number?"

Cheryl recited the phone number and I typed it into my phone. *Here goes nothing*, I thought to myself. I had no idea what I would say to them.

"When they answer, just tell them that I'm sorry for hurting them and I hope they can forgive me," Cheryl said as the phone rang.

A click sounded on the other end.

"Hello?" said a deep male voice.

"Hi, my name is Mellow Summers. I know your daughter Cheryl…"

Click.

He hung up on me. I couldn't believe it. The least he could have done was listen to what I had to say about his daughter.

I tapped the redial button on my phone.

"Hello?" said the same male voice.

"Look," I said, "I know your daughter, Cheryl, and she would like…"

Click.

He hung up on me again.

I glanced at Cheryl who faded in and out. If she had tear ducts, I'm certain that she would be crying.

I tried a third time and didn't wait for him to say "hello" when he answered. The moment I heard the click, I started speaking. "Cheryl just wanted me to tell—"

"Now you listen here," he yelled at me, "if you call here one more time, I will call the police and have them arrest you for harassment!"

"But what about your daughter?" I demanded. "She wishes to—"

"I have no daughter." He hung up.

Cheryl and I locked eyes and I knew that she was hurt, but had no idea of what I could do. I started to dial again, but Cheryl stopped me.

"It's okay. I didn't really think that my father would want to hear from me, but it was worth a try. I just wanted to tell them that I love them and am sorry for causing them so much pain."

Determined to get her message through somehow, I grabbed a piece of paper and a pen. "Just dictate what you want to say and I'll write it in a letter and mail it to them."

Cheryl's face brightened a little as words rushed from her mouth, eager to get out after having been bottled up inside for so long. For the next 20 minutes I wrote down what Cheryl wanted to say to her parents. Once done, I recopied the letter so that it would look neater and not so rushed, while also taking the time to correct any spelling mistakes, signed her name to it, and sealed it in an envelope addressed to her parents. I didn't know if they would open it or not, but I hoped that they would and at least read what she had wanted to tell them.

"Is there anything else you need me to do?" I asked.

"No," whispered Cheryl. "That was it."

Jackie stared at the both of us, an eager expression on her face.

"So what happens now?" I asked.

"I thought you knew," replied Cheryl, shrugging her shoulders.

No, I didn't. After all this time, I hadn't figured out

how a spirit knew to move on or not. Some just disappeared while others, like Rachel, hung around for an indefinite amount of time.

"Do you see a bright light?" asked Jackie with a hopeful note to her voice.

"No," Cheryl said.

"Let's not worry about it for right now," I said. "Perhaps it will work itself out later."

In her effort to clean up, Jackie knocked over the remote to the TV and it hit the power button, turning it on; and of all the channels it had to be tuned into, it was the midnight news.

"Authorities are still unsure of what caused the tiger to attack in the first place," said the reporter on the news.

Jackie reached for the remote and was about to turn the TV off when Cheryl stopped her.

"No, leave it, please."

"For now, the tiger has been segregated and is being kept in a cage, separate from the rest of the inhabitants of the circus with security guarding the entrance. Many are calling for the vicious ani—"

"He's not vicious!"

A man interrupted the reporter, flinging his arms, allowing his animated movements to make his point.

"You are all the vicious ones! That tiger would never harm anyone! Not unprovoked!"

Two circus performers yanked the man away from the reporter, urging him to calm down. I watched as he raised his arms and stalked off, kicking up a clump of dirt.

"As I was saying," continued the reporter, *"many are*

calling for the animal to be put down after its attack resulted in the death of this young woman."

A picture of Cheryl appeared on the screen just as Jackie shut off the TV. "That's enough of that," she said, "and I think we ought to call it a night."

I agreed, telling Cheryl that we were tired and needed sleep, but she didn't acknowledge me as she remained in a semisolid state, staring at the blank television screen. As I went to my bedroom, that sinking feeling that something more was going on filled my stomach.

Chapter 4

I awoke the next morning, still unable to shake the feeling that something more was going on. It didn't feel right that they were planning on putting the tiger down. Its attack made no sense. It had spent its life around people, and in environments such as a circus, people always perform with the tiger. They wouldn't allow one prone to lashing out at humans to be allowed in the circus. To add to it, Cheryl hadn't moved on, though part of that could be due to the fact that her father had hung up on me twice. I hoped he would at least read the letter I had written and put out to be mailed.

Seven in the morning.

I got dressed. It would be a while before the warehouse where I had to pick up the special candlesticks that Mr. Stilton had ordered would open, but there was no reason why I couldn't stop by the circus and have a chat with the tiger's trainer. If anything, he could answer a few questions for me and clear up some of the confusion about the animal's attack.

When I entered the kitchen, Jackie already stood there with three disposable "To Go" cups, filled with coffee and trails of steam hovering above them. I paused, gaping at her and how she had beaten me to the punch. She must have known what I was planning even before I did. "What's all this?"

"I saw that look on your face after watching that news program last night. I knew you wouldn't let this go until you at least had done some minor investigating on your own." She dumped a sugar packet in one of the cups of coffee. "Greg will be here any second."

A knock sounded at the door and in walked Greg.

"See? Told you." She handed him the coffee that she had just put the sugar into and Greg took it, thanking her, before taking a sip.

"All prepped and ready to go," he said as he walked over to me and gave me a kiss.

"I thought you had to go into work today," I said to him.

"One of the guys at work owed me a favor, so I switched shifts with him and go in later."

I looked around, noticing that Cheryl was nowhere to be seen.

"What's wrong?" asked Greg.

"I don't see Cheryl."

"Maybe she moved on," said Jackie with a hopeful note to her voice.

Though I wished that were true, I had a feeling that Cheryl hadn't moved on at all, but had just disappeared for the moment. "Perhaps," I replied. "We should go."

We grabbed our coffee and hurried down the stairs to the main floor where the parking area to the complex was and took my car in case Mr. Stilton's order also consisted of a few items that tended to be messy, which had happened in the past, and I preferred that it be my car that got dirty instead of someone else's.

We arrived at the circus within 30 minutes, due to me speeding just a little and taking a few back roads so as to avoid rush hour traffic, and the police. I parked away from the main area.

"So where do you think they're keeping the tiger?" I asked.

"It could be that place with all of the added security," Jackie pointed at a compound with uniformed security guards standing around it. Okay. Missing the obvious there, Mel. I crawled out of the car, unsure of how I was going to talk my way into the tiger's prison, but as luck would have it, I didn't have to, because at that moment, I spotted the tiger's trainer as he filled a bucket with water, recognizing his bulky form from the news program that had been on last night.

"Excuse me!" I ran up to him.

He paused, turning around and giving me a quizzical and doubtful look.

"Excuse me!" I hurried after him, with Jackie and Greg close behind, when he turned and tried to walk away. "I want to talk to you about your tiger."

The man stopped and whirled around to face me, his

face flushed with anger. "Look," he spat, "I don't care who you are, but I'll not allow you to go in there and take pictures so you can post it on your blog."

"What... No, I don't want that at all," I said, taken aback by his confrontational demeanor. "I don't think the tiger did this on purpose."

The man's face softened.

At that moment two stacked crates fell over, spilling masks, dumbbells, and bungee cords. Jackie hurried over to it, pretending that she had been the one to knock it over. "Oops. Sorry," she said with a fake smile.

Guess who had just arrived. Though I couldn't see her, I suspected that Cheryl had followed us and was trying to remain inconspicuous, except that her tendency to knock things over, even in death, gave away her presence.

The man stared at us, ready to throw us out if I didn't say something quick to convince him to talk to us.

"I'm Mel," I said, introducing myself, "and this is Jackie and Greg. We were here yesterday when the Tiger atta—"

The man's brows furrowed and I knew I had to be careful about which words I used.

"—broke loose and that acrobat died."

His face softened again. "Poor Cheryl," he said. "She didn't deserve to go like that. She was a nice girl."

"I don't think the tiger did it on purpose," I continued. "Something about this doesn't make sense and we would like to talk to you about it, if you're willing, and maybe..."

"You want to prove the tiger's innocence?" asked the trainer.

"Yes," I replied, thinking that if I had let him believe that that was what we were there for, then he would let us in.

"Follow me," said thee trainer, leading us to the small compound where the tiger was.

"You really think they will let us in there?" asked Jackie, pointing at the two security guards.

"They will. I'm the only one who isn't afraid to go in there and feed Rocky."

"Rocky?" asked Greg.

"It's what I named the tiger," the trainer replied.

We all walked up to the two security guards who stopped us, just like we thought they would.

"Where do you think you're going?" demanded one of the guards.

"Where do you think?" retorted the trainer; the bucket of water sloshed in his hands.

"You're not taking them in there."

"They're with me," said the trainer, but the security guard just folded his arms, determined not to back down. "I need their help today, or would you rather I not feed the tiger and let him get hungry? He might get a bit unpredictable then."

The trainer's words had the desired effect. The security guard backed down and I guessed that he had envisioned what could happen to his chances of keeping his job if the tiger were to become agitated. "Ten minutes."

He stepped aside, motioning for his partner to do the same, allowing us to pass. We walked into the makeshift bunker, which was just a building that the circus had commandeered while in town and stuck a cage in there to keep the tiger in. A table moved as I stepped passed it and I glared at it, certain that Chery was there, but remaining invisible. I shared a look with Jackie while Greg tried hard to prevent himself from asking the question on his mind. I guess Jackie hadn't told him about our ghostly visitor last night, or at least, not about her tendency towards clumsiness.

"So, what is your interest in all of this?" asked the tiger trainer.

"Mr.…" I began, but allowed my voice to trail off.

"Ramone," replied the trainer, "my name is Ramone."

"Ramone," I said again, "I'm sort of a private investigator and some interested parties are not convinced that the tiger is responsible for yesterday's incident."

"What parties?"

"I can't disclose that. The thing is, the tiger is kept locked up, is he not?"

Ramone nodded. "He's kept in his cage at all times, like all of the animals we have. We keep them separated and those that are considered more dangerous are kept locked in steel cages in accordance with state regulations." He shook the steel bars to demonstrated how sturdy they were. "This is reinforced steel. I made a point of showing it to the authorities just so they would let Rocky stay here."

I did my best not to make a comment about someone naming a tiger after a movie about boxing. I had more important things to do. The tiger looked up from its toy and rolled over on its back, lifting its front paws into the air, purring up a storm. "He doesn't look dangerous," I said.

"He's not!" The defensive tone in the trainer's voice told me to be careful of my choice of words.

"I didn't mean—"

"This tiger wouldn't hurt anyone. Not unprovoked. You can pet him if you like."

When no one moved, the trainer reached through the bars and stroked the tiger's nose. "See? He's harmless. Come on."

He snatched my hand and shoved it through the bars. I tried to pull back, but the man had an iron grip and before I knew it, my arm was halfway through the bars. Doing my best not to shake or show my fear, I held my hand as steady as I could while the tiger sniffed it with its cold, wet nose, coating it with a thin film of mucous. The tiger pressed against my hand, rubbing its chin against it; it's purr grew louder until the soft rumbling resonated off the surrounding walls. I wriggled my fingers. The tiger's purr grew even more as he continued to rub against them. He didn't seem dangerous at all. Feeling more brave, I stroked the top of the tiger's head, remarking at how soft and silky his fur was.

Ramone chuckled. "He likes you."

"His fur is so soft," I said.

"Yeah, well, I feed him right. Make sure he gets plenty of proteins and fats with the appropriate amount of vegetables. Tigers are carnivores so they need meat, but Rocky here has a sweet tooth for carrots."

The tiger pawed at my hand in a playful manner, but he kept his claws retracted and never touched me with more than a gentle pat.

"He likes you," said Ramone.

"So I don't understand," said Jackie, amazed at how the tiger was so gentle, "why would he attack all those people yesterday?"

"Something must have provoked him," Greg replied.

"You're right about that," said Ramone, standing up while I continued to pet the tiger. "Animals, by their nature, will not attack a human. They only do it for three reasons: they feel threatened, are starving, or you get too close to their cubs. Well, he's got no cubs, and I feed him three times a day so he isn't starving, which means the only other option is that he felt threatened, but I don't know how that could be."

"Why is that?" asked Greg.

"Rocky loves people. He's been raised around them. I raised him myself. Taught him to be gentle."

"But yesterday he—"

"I know what happened yesterday. Sometimes every animal likes to play and sometimes they get a little rough. You can't be around large ones like this tiger without getting a few scratches, but I trained him so that all I had to do was say a particular word or clap my hands when he starts acting up and he'd settle down. The other problem is that tigers can't unlock cages."

Ramone grabbed a padlock from the counter in the room and showed it to us. "This is what I use on the pens that keep the animals contained. Now you tell me how that tiger unlocked it."

I looked at the lock—it was the size of my hand—examining it, wondering how anyone could have opened it without the key or a pair of lock cutters. "I don't know."

"Exactly." Ramone slammed the lock back on the counter. "This was what was used to lock the tiger's pen yesterday. I know because I was the one that locked it.

I'm in charge of the animals and always make sure that they are contained and can't get out. There isn't a mark on the lock and I have the key right here."

I glanced at Jackie and Greg and knew we all thought the same thing: how did the tiger get out?

"Those idiots," Ramone raged, "want to put Rocky down because they think he is a dangerous animal, but none of them are interested in what really happened. I raised that tiger since he was a cub. He'd never attack anyone without provocation."

A bag crinkled in the room and I glanced over to see Greg pull a small bag of chips from his pocket. "Sorry," he mumbled over a mouthful of chips, "forgot to eat breakfast."

I grinned as I thought about how he's developing some of my bad habits; I didn't always remember to eat. A loud crunch echoed as he bit into another chip.

The tiger's ears perked up and the animal jumped up, reaching through the bars of the cage with soft growls, rattling the side of the pen with each movement he made.

"What's wrong with him?" asked Jackie, backing away.

Ramone snatched the bag of chips from Greg, bringing it to his nose, taking a big sniff. "Coconut," he mumbled.

"They're new," said Greg, "so I thought I would give them a try."

I watched as the tiger reached for the bag of chips in the trainer's hand. "Why is he doing that?"

Ramone handed the chips back to Greg and snapped his fingers, creating a loud popping sound which forced the tiger to jerk back and sit on its haunches.

"How'd you…" I began.

"I told you," answered Ramone, glancing back at me before turning back to the tiger, "you have to know how to train them. He knows that when I snap my fingers or clap my hands he supposed to settle down."

I looked at the tiger who still eyed Greg's bag of coconut chips with longing, but remained seated, though his twitching whiskers gave away his desire to go after the chips. "I take it that he really likes chips."

"Not really," said Ramone, "but he likes coconut."

"Seriously?" said Jackie.

"He has a sweet tooth for carrots, but this insatiable desire for anything coconut, almost like he's addicted to them. Like people, every animal has its quirks. Guess this is his."

"So, would he harm someone to get coconuts?" I asked.

"Nah," said Ramone. "He gets a little pushy when he smells them, but like I've said, I've got him trained to sit if he hears me snapping my fingers or—"

"We get the point," interrupted Jackie.

"Would Cheryl have known about the coconuts?" I asked.

"Not sure. It's possible. Most are aware of it, but Rocky here wasn't supposed to go out in the ring for his performance until the afternoon, so if anyone was wearing a lotion with that scent, they would have been gone long before his act."

The tiger continued to give a pleading look to Ramone, but he twirled his index finger and the animal padded to a corner and laid down, placing his head on his front paws. A speck of brown against the white part of his paw caught my attention and I remembered seeing something similar yesterday in the ring after Cheryl had been killed. "What's that on his paws?" I asked, pointing at the discoloration.

Ramone looked at it, his eyes lighting up, and walked to a corner in the room where he pulled out a metallic container. "This," he said, holding it up for us to see. "With all the sand and sawdust around, even his paws get dry and cracked. This is some specialized cream I have that I put on his pads every night. It moistens the skin there—just like how you would put hand cream on your cracked knuckles in the wintertime."

He unscrewed the lid and dipped his pinky finger in, pulling it out so that we all could see that it was covered in brown goo that hung in swaying strings. "Sometimes I put some on him in the morning, especially right before a show. It does leave a bit of a residue, but it keeps the pads of his paws soft."

Well, that explained the brown spots I had seen on the ground in the ring.

Two whips that had been hanging from the wall dropped to the floor with a clatter, followed by a soft "Oooh".

Ramone turned towards it, his brows scrunched together, and I knew he was thinking that something wasn't quite right.

"I think we ought to get going," I said, hoping Cheryl would leave the room before she knocked something else over, but as luck would have it, a chair scooted and toppled over, before shifting again.

"Sorry," Cheryl whispered, but in this room every little noise carried and I knew, judging by the confused expression on Ramone's face, that he had heard her.

"We thank you for your time," I said to Ramone, while shoving Jackie and Greg out the door before he could ask us about the mysterious disembodied voice that seemed to be knocking things over. I didn't want to have to explain to him that Cheryl's ghost still hung around the circus.

"So, what next?" asked Jackie.

I pulled us behind some barrels so that I could talk to Cheryl, who remained behind us, sending a wave of falling stacks of props, hay, and crates with each passing second. "Cheryl," I said and the reign of tumbling items stopped, "Were you wearing anything with coconut in it?"

"Oh, I don't know," she replied. "I was given this cream for my face. The makeup we wear can really dry out our skin, so one of the other performers gave me this cream to put on before applying the makeup. It was supposed to help keep the skin moisturized and keep the makeup from sticking to it. Anyway, I think I remember it having a slight coconut smell, but I never thought too much about it."

"So that explains why the tiger went after her like it did," said Greg.

"But it doesn't explain much," replied Jackie.

"I need to see the body," I blurted out to which Jackie choked on a wad of spit.

"You want to what?" she said.

"I need to see the body," I replied.

"As in, go to the morgue?"

"That is the general idea."

"You're—"

"I think I know a way we can get in there," Greg interrupted her.

"You are not seriously supporting her on this!" Jackie placed her hands on her slender hips, doing her best to appear threatening, but it wasn't working.

"I don't think you're going to be able to talk her out of it—"

"You know I am standing right here," I said, but they ignored me.

"—and I think Mel's right: we need to examine the body."

Sand shifted next to us and I remembered that Cheryl had been standing there the entire time, listening to us."

"Cheryl," I began, even though she remained invisible," I'm sorry…"

"No, no, it' quite all right. I'll meet you all there and do my best to not cause a scene."

Though she had never solidified while at the circus, I knew Cheryl had gone—just one of those feelings you get.

"She…" began Jackie with hesitation.

"She left," I replied. "I don't have much time until I need to pick up those candlesticks."

We piled into my car and I hurried, while remaining aware of the speed traps along the way, to the morgue, while trying to devise a plan for how we would get ourselves in there. We settled on Greg distracting the Medical Examiner somehow. I found a place to park that was out of the way. I didn't need anyone recognizing my car and getting word back to Detective Shorts about what I was up to, not that he would have been surprised.

"Mel!"

I whirled around at the sound of someone shriek-
ing my name only to be accosted by a streaking blur of
fuzzy, electric chartreuse humanoid shape crashing into me
and squishing me against the door to my car. The impact,
slammed my car door shut and knocked the wind out me,
leaving me heaving for more air, though I ended up gagging
on the fuzzy pieces of lint that escaped from the blouse.

"I'm so glad I followed you." Tammy's voice spilled
from the chartreuse eyesore. The bright sun glared off
the horrible color—a road sign looked dull and pale in
comparison—blinding anyone who dared to look at it
without a pair of sunglasses.

"I can't breathe," I gasped as Greg yanked Tammy off me.

I stared at Tammy as she stood before me in another
of her outrageous outfits, that she had made herself. The
sleeveless blouse, which looked as though it had been
knitted from some sort of fuzzy yarn, which shedded
worse than my mom's long haired dog, attacked my eyes
with its neon glow that grew in intensity by the second.
Below the shirt was a plum purple skirt, store bought,
but modified by Tammy with crocheted flowers dotting
the hemline, which wouldn't have been so bad, except
that the flowers were a mixture of neon pink and orange,
encased in more of the awful chartreuse.

"What are you doing here?" I asked her, shading my eyes
from her glowing outfit, while Jackie put on her sunglasses.

"I followed you!" Tammy jumped up and down all
excited that she had managed to follow us without being
noticed, and I had to admit that I had no idea she had
been right behind us.

"Did you lose your way to the insane asylum?" Jackie quipped.

Lucky for us, Tammy hadn't heard her, still overjoyed at having managed to follow us around town without ever being caught. "I knew you wouldn't let this drop. You are a super sleuth—"

Jackie snorted at that statement.

"—and it is up to you, with my help, to solve this case!"

"I don't know about the super part," I said, "but I will admit that there are a few things I think are odd about Che—that poor woman's death."

"So you are investigating on your own!" Tammy jumped up and down, clapping her hands with exuberance as her smile broadened. "I knew it!"

"Uh… yeah, we need to go and time is running short," said Jackie in a semi-hostile tone to Tammy, who never noticed it. Jackie had never gotten over the fireworks display incident from two years ago when Tammy, in her effort to spice up my fourth of July display at the Candle Shoppe, had taped sparklers to the table and lit them, which resulted in almost setting the place on fire and the fire department being called. It was one of her more insane moments, but not her last.

Tammy nodded her head at Jackie, staring at her wide-eyed and full of excitement, not getting, or refusing to understand, Jackie's hidden message.

"Would you like to join us, Tammy?" I asked, giving Jackie a look, telling her to just let it go. She huffed, but remained silent.

"Yes!" shrieked Tammy, hopping from foot to foot in a vain attempt to contain her excitement.

"All right, then," I said, hoping that Tammy's presence wouldn't ruin our chances of getting into the morgue as she had a way of allowing her impulses to dictate her actions, "we need a distraction. None of us are supposed to be in there and we don't need the medical examiner catching us."

Greg opened the passenger door to my car and pulled out a half empty bottle of Coke. He unscrewed the lid and poured some of the now flat liquid into his hands before splashing it on his hair.

"What are you doing?" asked Jackie as we watched him work the sticky substance through his hair, forming a few spikes and giving himself a frazzled look.

"Providing your distraction," answered Greg as he untucked his shirt, making it look rumpled and unkempt. "Most people act a little crazy or out of sorts when someone they know has died or gotten hurt. I'll go in first, looking like this and pretend that I've lost someone while you three sneak into the room where the bodies are kept. You won't have long, so be quick."

The medical examiner's office, though part of the police department, had its own entrance as well so those coming to identify a body didn't have to walk through the main department and past the people who had been brought in for various misdemeanors or arrests, but there was a stairwell connecting the two. We all headed over to the main doors, but Greg went in first while the rest of us waited. I looked around for Cheryl, but she hadn't shown up, or if she was there, she remained invisible. We watched through the glass in the door, doing our best to keep out of sight while I glanced around in case anyone else showed up.

"You have to help me," Greg said, acting all breathless and agitated.

The medical examiner looked up from her paperwork and looked at Greg with a concerned expression as he leaned on the counter as though he needed its help in supporting his weight.

"What can I do for you, sir?" asked the medical examiner, her voice soft and calm.

"They said… they said that they brought her in here," Greg sobbed and he had fake tears to go with it. Who knew he was such a good actor?

"Whom have they brought in?" The medical examiner placed her paperwork on the counter, her attention focused on Greg and his frazzled demeanor.

"My sister!"

I took another glance around, but so far no one had bothered to try and walk through the main doors to the ME's office.

"Can I have her name?" The woman remained calm, no doubt doing her best to not agitate Greg any further.

"Um…" Greg sniffled through some fake tears. Man, was he good. "Lily Babama."

Babama? Okay, he obviously did not think that one through.

"Lily Babama?" asked the medical examiner.

"Lily Hossel. Babama was a nickname."

The medical examiner woke up the computer and scrolled through a list of names, but as her face turned to one of puzzlement, I knew that she was about to discover our ruse, or at least assume that Greg might have assumed the worst. Greg must have sensed it too because at that moment, he broke down into a rack of sobbing, forcing the poor woman to tear herself away from the computer, snatch a box of tissues, and lead Greg away from the front desk to a set of chairs in the far corner.

"Why don't we sit over here for a moment," she suggested, sounding calm and concerned.

Greg motioned us to come inside as he and the medical examiner walked away. I tore open the door, thankful that there were no bells or anything on there, and ushered Jackie and Tammy inside, hurrying down the hall. A missing member of our group stopped me. Tammy had paused in the hallway, watching Greg as he continued to play the part of a man who thought someone special to him had died. She raised her hands and was about to applaud his performance when I snatched her left wrist and wrenched her away, whispering, "Come on."

I shoved them through a set of double doors, which led into another hallway lined with metallic doors, each with a small window within them, on both sides. I glanced around, but had no idea where to begin.

"Now what?" asked Jackie.

"I guess we just pick one and hope we get lucky," I replied as another corner of my brain wondered where Cheryl had gone to and why she hadn't shown up yet.

I pointed at the first set of doors on our right and went through them, still clasping Tammy's wrist. The sterile room with its empty gurneys, rubber tubes wrapped in neat coils around metal hooks, and folded sheets told me that no corpse had been in there for a while. I motioned for Jackie to follow me back into the hallway, while still dragging Tammy to keep her from doing something crazy, and went through the second set of doors on the right.

In front of us stood a gurney with a body, whose form I recognized, with a sheet draped over it, covering it from the chest down. As I examined the corpse, I could tell that it had already had an autopsy performed on it. The telltale scar on the chest with fresh thread sewn through it to hold it together gave it away. Tammy went limp and I released my grip on her.

"Are you okay?" I asked, worried about her paled complexion and concerned that she might become sick.

"The smell is getting to me," she said, putting her hand over her nose and mouth.

I helped her over to the sink in the room, having not paid much attention to the hospital smell that saturated the area. "Stand over here if you feel like you're going to throw up."

Tammy leaned over the stainless steel sink and splashed some cold water on her face as I wandered over to where Jackie was. "Find anything?" I asked her.

"Not much," replied Jackie. "There's a few charts here, but I can't decipher the shorthand or the notes. It does appear as though they ran the standard toxicity screen, but I'm not sure what all this means."

I took the charts from her and studied them myself, knowing that I would need a little help in understanding what was written on them. I spotted the only computer in the room and went over to it. A login window asking for a username and password filled the screen when I wriggled the mouse, which didn't surprise me. I pulled out my phone.

"What are you doing?" asked Jackie.

"Calling Jack," I replied as I pressed the call button next to his picture; it was one I had snapped some months ago while he chewed on a chili dog. Not one of his more flattering moments.

"Mel, I'm really not in the mood," Jack said when he answered, making me wish that he didn't have caller ID, since his already knowing it was me on the phone caught me off-guard.

"I need your help," I said in a soft voice.

"You always need my help."

"Yeah, but I need your help to access a computer."

That piqued his interest. "A computer? Really? Wait... why are you whispering?"

And here we go. "No reason."

Jackie tapped her watch, telling me that I needed to hurry up.

"Where are you?"

"At the morgue," I replied.

"And you want me to help you break into their computer?"

"Yep."

"Where's Greg?"

"In the lobby giving the medical examiner a sob story about his sister."

"He doesn't have a sis—oh, never mind."

A scalpel shifted on its own followed by a voice saying, "Why did they put that there?"

Cheryl had arrived.

Jackie placed her forehead in the palm of her hand, no doubt thinking the same thing I was: oh, no.

"Type in admin for the username," said Jack and I did as instructed. "Now in the password area type in 8@65TU*9PQ. That's the ME's passcode."

"And you know this how?" I asked.

"I gave it to her when I installed the new database software on the computer. She's supposed to change it to something else, but chances are, she hasn't. Most people don't."

"How would she even remember it?"

"She probably has it written down someplace. What are you looking for anyway?"

"You know that woman that died at the circus yesterday? Well…"

"I should have known. Is there anything else you need?"

I scanned through the report, which, unlike the chart on the table, had been typed up with complete words, not shorthand. "I'm not seeing anything in here that indicates she was murdered, except the report says that she died of asphyxiation, but she was mauled by a tiger."

I heard keys clacking on the other end of the phone and guessed that Jack looked up the same autopsy report. "Odd," he said and I pictured him leaning close to the computer screen while holding a half-empty soda can in his hand.

"How could she have died of asphyxiation"—I walked over to Cheryl's body and examined some of the scars from the tiger's claws, noting the same discoloration on her skin that matched what was on the animal's paws—"when everyone saw her get attacked by a tiger?"

Jack released a long exhale into the mouthpiece of the phone in response.

I went back to the computer, but couldn't decipher most of what had been typed in. "Did they run a toxicology report?"

"If you look at the right hand column of the report, you will see that they ran a standard one and everything came up negative, except that they did find residue of a substance in her system, but were unable to identify it."

"Unable or just didn't bother?"

"Probably a little bit of both," said Jack. "Whatever it was isn't showing up in the normal tox screen, and I'm guessing that the ME just didn't see a reason to run any further tests to try and identify the unknown substance."

"I'm not finding a cause of death on here, yet she already noted that the person asphyxiated," I said as I looked more closely at the report.

"That's because the ME hasn't made an official ruling on it, yet. Either she is planning to run more tests, or is unsure of what to put due to all of the attention this particular death is getting. There is a lot of pressure from the department heads to have her rule it as death by tiger."

I took another look at the claw marks, but just as I had noted the day before, they were too superficial to have caused her death and would not have caused her to asphyxiate. "Why don't they want to investigate this further?"

"Circuses are fun for the average public, but trouble for local police," replied Jack. "The last thing they want is the murder of some out of town circus performer that remains unsolved. It's bad press and the police commissioner is running for re-election this year. This sort of incident, if ruled a murder, and if left unsolved, could result in bad publicity for him."

"Politics before murder," I muttered.

"Something like that."

Jackie's frantic waving forced me to look up from the computer screen. "What?" I mouthed.

"Tammy's missing," she whispered.

I looked at where I had left her, having forgotten that she was with us, and there was no sign of Tammy. "What?" I said out loud, forgetting where I was for the moment, my voice echoing around the room.

"Jack, I have to go." I hung up and logged out of the computer, hoping that when the medical examiner logged onto her computer again she wouldn't notice that someone else had been browsing through her files.

"Where did she go?" I asked Jackie.

"I don't know," Jackie replied. "I turned away from her for a moment and she was gone!"

I groaned. The last thing we needed was for Tammy to get lost in the city morgue when we weren't supposed to be there in the first place. "We need to find her now."

We rushed out of the room and into the hallway, looking up and down it, but saw no sign of where Tammy might have gone. I pointed at a door that sat ajar and both Jackie and I ran to it, bursting into the room, but there was still no Tammy. A clatter echoed from the adjoining room and I cringed as I thought about how that would attract some unwanted attention.

Once again, Jackie and I ran through a set of double doors, charging into the adjoining room where we found Tammy standing on a chair with a sternal saw in her hands.

"Tammy!" I hissed.

"Hey, guys," she replied in a cheery voice.

"What are you doing?" I demanded, though I had a feeling that I could guess.

"Look what I found." Tammy pressed the power button to the sternal saw and waved it all around with a huge smile on her face, thinking that this was all some sort of game. It's high-pitched, buzzing sound filled the room and I knew this was going to garner someone's notice. "It's one of those saw thingies!"

She released the power button, to which I was thankful as I feared that she might actually hurt herself, and jumped off the chair. "Hey, do you think there is a body around here I can use this on. I always wanted to carve up a corpse like they do on CSI."

"Put that down. Now!" I yelled at her, while trying to keep my voice low at the same time.

Tammy's face fell as the excitement of her living out one of her dreams flittered away.

"These aren't toys," said Jackie in a gentler tone, something I had not heard her use on Tammy before. Maybe she was as afraid as I was that the girl would hurt herself, and neither of us wanted to make an emergency trip to the hospital.

"I thought I heard it come from here," came a distant, female voice.

A sudden hot flash raced up my spine and soaked my

collarbone as I realized that the one thing I wanted to avoid was marching up to meet me. We were going to get caught.

"Miss Evanick?"

I froze. That was Detective Shorts' voice. There was no way I was going to be able to explain my way out of this one if he caught me.

"Yes?" replied the medical examiner.

"I need your report on the victim of the tiger attack that took place yesterday," replied Detective Shorts.

"Um, yes, this way."

My eyes darted from crevice to crevice in the room as I searched for a place to hide all three of us. While I tried to think of what to do, Tammy decided that it was the perfect time to pick up a bone saw. She held it up with a wide smile, her eyes wide with excitement. I almost lunged for her, but Jackie was closer and snatched the saw from her, dropping it on the table, which produced another clatter, before seizing Tammy's arm and dragging her away from the medical instruments.

"What do we do?" mouthed Jackie.

I spotted the wall of square doors going from floor to ceiling and turned to Jackie as she guessed what I was thinking.

"No!" she hissed.

I bolted over to one of the cold chambers to open it, but stopped when I noticed that another had already been opened and the head of the body inside poked out of it. I pulled it into the light and frowned. Someone had put neon pink lipstick on it's blue lips, orange blush on its pallid cheeks, and green mascara on the eyelashes.

"What is this?" I asked Tammy as she shifted from foot to foot while nibbling on her index finger.

"She looked a little pale," she said. "So I put some makeup on her to liven up her appearance."

The footsteps drew closer.

"Something tells me it's about to get lively in here all right," said Jackie.

I pushed the corpse back into its cold chamber and opened another one. Empty. Good. I motioned for either Jackie or Tammy to get inside.

"You've got to be kidding," Jackie moaned.

"It's either this or get caught."

With her face pinched, and I knew just what she thought of me at that moment, Jackie dragged Tammy over and pushed her to the empty cold chamber.

"Hey—What!" Tammy started to protest, but stopped.

Jackie opened her mouth to explain, but—and to my astonishment and disbelief—Tammy's face lit up with exuberance when she realized what we were trying to do.

"I've always wanted to be in one of these," she said as she crawled inside the cold chamber. I shut the door behind her, wondering if I should just leave her there.

"Sometimes I worry about her," said Jackie.

I opened another cold chamber and looked at Jackie.

"You so owe me," she mumbled as she crawled inside and I closed the door.

I pried open a door to a third cold chamber—thank goodness it was empty too—and slipped inside, closing it just enough to conceal me, but where I could peek through a small slit, just as another tray with medical instruments fell over and the medical examiner and Detective Shorts walked in. I tried to look for Cheryl through the small opening, but saw no sign of her.

"Miss Evanick?" said Detective Shorts.

The medical examiner stood in the center of the autopsy room, looking around before turning to the detective. "Sorry," she apologized, "I thought I heard something."

"Miss Evanick," said Detective Shorts, "I don't mean to be rude, but I have other cases to get to and the sooner I can get this one—"

"Yes, I'm sorry."

I pulled the door a little closer to me when they approached the cold chambers. As I did so, I noticed a speck of chartreuse green poking out of the one next to me and it clashed against the stainless steel siding just like blood on new-fallen snow. Why did Tammy have to wear that outlandish shirt? Dead bodies don't wear knitted clothes and they especially do not wear that awful color. Sweat dripped down the sides of my temples, pooling on the metallic slab beneath me as I clung to the edges of the door, hoping that no one noticed that dot of color against gray.

"The victim suffered from multiple cuts from the tiger's claws, though they were all superficial. None of them are the cause of death. I ran the standard toxicology test, but it came up negative, except for one unknown substance, which I haven't been able to identify. It's pretty minute, so I have my doubts that it has anything to do with cause of death."

"If you have been unable to identify it, then how do you know if it's important or not?"

"I…"

"I'd like you to run some more tests," said Detective Shorts, "see if you can identify this unknown substance."

"But, Detective, the captain has asked me—"

"I'm aware of what the captain wants and I know that he, the police commissioner, and the mayor would like to be rid of this case by tomorrow, if not sooner. Run the tests."

"Yes, sir."

"Where's the body?"

"In the other room."

"Then, why did you bring me in here?"

"As I said, I thought I had heard something."

"Will you, please, show me the body?"

"Yes, of course. This way."

As the medical examiner led Detective Shorts to the other room, a tremendous crash filled the hallway, coming straight from the front desk. Both Detective Shorts and the medical examiner rushed from the room to see what had caused the commotion. Wasting no time, I shoved the door open and jumped out of the cold chamber. I ran to the one Jackie was in and yanked it open.

She gasped as I helped her out. "That was too close. Let's get out of here before they come back."

I didn't argue. I hurried to the chamber I had locked Tammy in and heaved its door open, but instead of being greeted with relieved gasps, I was met with shouts of joy.

"That was fun!" said Tammy as she crawled out, her feet making harsh clacks on the linoleum floor when she stood up. "We should do that again. I don't think I have ever been in a more peaceful place. I could have taken a nap in there."

"Does she not know what normally goes in these things?" Jackie whispered in my left ear.

Detective Shorts' and the medical examiner's voices prickled my ears. I ushered Jackie and Tammy to the set of double doors, opening one ajar so that I could peek out. They headed straight for us. Before I had time to think of a plan, they walked into the room next door which had Cheryl's body in it. I breathed a sigh of relief, but wasted no time in pushing Tammy and Jackie out the door. We tiptoed down the hallway, past the examination room they were in, and bolted through the doors into the lobby, heading straight for the exit without bothering to acknowledge the confused looks of an older couple who had just walked in, glad to be out of there.

I glanced at my watch. Oh, my goodness! It was 8:30 and I still had to grab that box from the warehouse for Mr. Stilton. "Is there any way you two can make your way back?" I asked. "I still have to grab that box of candlesticks."

Jackie checked her watch and gasped. "Goodness, Mel! I can't believe how long that took. You need to go!"

"I want to come!" Tammy tried to follow me to my car, but Jackie seized her around the collar and yanked her back.

"You're going home."

Tammy slumped her shoulders.

"Greg, I…"

"Don't worry about it," said Greg. "Go do what you need to. I'll just borrow Jack's car. Besides, I need to get ready for work anyway."

"Thanks." I kissed Greg and left.

Chapter 5

I arrived at the local warehouse that had the specialty candlestick holders that Mr. Stilton had ordered, easing my car around parked semis as I made my way to the visitors' parking area. He had worked out an arrangement with the management of the warehouse where if he picked up his special orders, he got a five percent discount; except this time he wasn't able to pick up the order himself. I didn't mind. The trip gave me a chance to think about Cheryl and where she might have trotted off to. After the morgue—though she never materialized, I had an inkling that she was there—she seemed to have disappeared. I didn't have to worry for long. As I pulled into a parking space, the back of the passenger seat fell backward, slamming into the backseat.

"Sorry," mumbled the disembodied voice of Cheryl.

"It's okay," I replied.

She solidified a little, but continued to fade in and out.

"Where did you go?"

"Nowhere," said Cheryl.

"Was that you who caused the crash in the lobby?" I asked, putting the car into park and shutting off the engine.

"Yeah. I didn't mean to make such a mess, though. I just wanted to help you all out."

"Make a mess?" In the rush to get out of there, I never bothered to look for the source of the crash.

"Well," replied Cheryl, turning a pale shade of pink, which surprised me because I didn't think ghosts could blush, "I meant to only knock the stapler to the ground, but it had gotten caught on the mouse to the computer. They didn't have one of those wireless ones and it snagged the cord which had gotten tangled around the monitor to the computer. So, when I knocked the stapler off the counter, it took the mouse with it, which also caused the monitor to tip over."

That explained the loud crash. "It doesn't sound so bad," I said.

"But that isn't the worst part."

"The worst part?"

"When the monitor tipped over, it hit a coffee cup, which knocked it over. Coffee spilled everywhere and most of it got on the tower to the computer. A few sparks flew and I was so afraid of the possibility of a fire that I went for the fire extinguisher."

I strained to keep a straight face. "And what happened after that?"

"It slipped—I haven't quite figured out how to grab things in this new form—and it crashed to the floor, but, somehow, the pin popped from its hold and white foam went everywhere."

My tongue ached from me biting it so hard to keep from laughing. It was almost like her accident was straight from a humorous movie. "I thank you for helping us to get out of there. Now, I need to go in here and pick up something for my boss and get to work. Do you think you can wait here?"

"I'd rather come with you," said Cheryl.

A part of me cringed at the thought of bringing her in. Her track record of causing a scene was well-known, but I didn't want to be rude. "Sure," I said.

"What did you find out in that place anyway?" asked Cheryl as I opened the car door and stuck my left foot out.

I flopped back in my seat, unsure if I should tell her then or later. I decided to just tell her because later had a habit of never showing up. "I think you were murdered."

Silence loomed over us as Cheryl's face fell and she stared at her ethereal hands. I didn't know what I could say to comfort her and I still had to get that box for Mr. Stilton, so I hopped out of the car. When I turned around to assure her that I would find out who did it, she had gone, and I had no way of knowing if she had just vanished or was going to follow me into the lobby of the warehouse.

I glanced at my watch and sighed, knowing I would be late for work as I ran into the front lobby of the warehouse.

"May I help you?" asked a bored desk clerk who looked

as though she much preferred spending time texting or fiddling with social media on her phone than doing her job.

"I'm here to pick up the special order by Mr. Stilton from the Candle Shoppe."

The clerk released an exasperated sigh, drowned out by the banging sounds of the machinery in the next room. "You were supposed to pick it up yesterday."

"Mr. Stilton wasn't able to and asked me to come in this morning to get it."

"You know, when we have to hold on to something for you, it means that we can't spare the space to hold on to another order for another client."

Geez, what did this lady eat for breakfast? Did somebody put cream of bitchiness in her coffee this morning? "I'm here now," I said, getting irritated and it showed in my voice. "Are you going to get it for me or should I go back there and get it myself?"

I glanced at the wall behind her and all of the shelves filled with bags and boxes, no doubt containing the orders from other clients, hoping that the one Mr. Stilton had asked me to get was there. A paper bag shifted on the top shelf followed by the black cardboard box next to it moving to the right. Before I knew it, not only did the box shoot out from the shelf, crashing on the floor next to the clerk's feet, but the bag next to it toppled off, followed by the entire shelf breaking free of the wall and smashing into the tiles below.

"Oops," came Cheryl's voice.

The clerk jumped out of her chair, taking three steps back as her eyes widened to the point there I thought they might pop out of her head. She stared at the shelf as it hung from the two bolts that still held it in place and swayed in the slight breeze coming from the vents above us.

"My order," I said, hoping to turn her attention away from the fact that the shelf had been knocked down by a ghost.

"Did you not see that?"

"The shelf fell. Most likely a few screws pulled loose because you had too much weight on it."

Cheryl must have decided to try and walk past the clerk because at that moment a bit of moving air not only created a slight chill in the room, but the clerk's phone, which had been teetering on the edge of the counter, clattered on the floor and snapped a picture. The clerk picked it up and dropped the phone on the counter jumping back in horror.

Unable to contain my curiosity, and having a bad feeling of what was on the phone, I picked it up and looked at its most recent photo. In it, you could make out the shimmer of Cheryl's circus outfit and faint outline of her face as a few bits of hair draped around it.

"Not my best side," whispered Cheryl in my ear as she leaned over me to glance at the picture.

I looked up and there she was, a full-bodied apparition. At first, I thought that perhaps she had made it where only I could see her, but one look at the clerk's shocked face told me that she saw Cheryl too. I nodded in her direction and Cheryl looked at her, realizing that everyone could see her. She turned to leave and just as she faded, her hand hit a pencil holder, knocking it over.

"Oh, dear," moaned Cheryl. "I wish I wasn't such a klutz."

"My box," I said to the clerk, jolting her out of her frozen state.

"Wha—yeah." She went to the phone and picked it up, pressing a number. "Joe, I need that box for Mr. Stilton. Yes, bring it to the front desk."

Within minutes, a man walked out, carrying a box that looked to be about half my size. As I stared at it, I tried to think of how I was going to carry it to my car. He dumped it on the counter and handed me a slip to sign before walking away.

"There's your box," snapped the clerk, returning to her bored and rude demeanor.

I smiled at her and picked up the box, almost collapsing from its weight and dropped it back on the counter. "Do you think you could get someone to help me with this?"

"Nope," said the clerk.

I turned to grab the box again but the clerk stopped me. "My phone?"

I had forgotten that I still held it. I took one last look at the snapshot of Cheryl and pressed the delete button before handing the woman her phone.

"Hey, what happened to the picture?" she screamed as she looked at her phone.

"Oops," I said and picked up the box and walked out the door.

Sweat dotted my face as I carried the cumbersome box (could it get any heavier?) my posture sagging with each step I took as I tried to hurry to my car. By the time I reached the trunk of my vehicle, I was dragging the hefty package. I dumped the box on the ground, wondering how I was going to lift it into my trunk. I settled on propping one edge on the bumper, hoping that I could somehow roll it up the back of the car until it fell into the open trunk.

"Do you want some help?" asked Cheryl, appearing by my side.

I paused, trying to imagine how I looked, sitting on the ground, using what little strength I had in my arms to heave the box into my car with a translucent figure of a woman standing next to me. "Um, sure," I gasped as a corner of the package pressed against my chin.

Cheryl reached down and took one end of the box, allowing me to stand up while I continued to hold my half, and together we heaved it into the trunk of my car, where it landed with a loud thud. I just hoped that I didn't damage anything in there.

"See," said Cheryl, "I'm not a total disaster."

I grinned. "Never thought you were."

I climbed into the driver's seat and motioned for Cheryl to get in, but she declined and disappeared. I wasn't worried about her wanting to leave and I knew I would see her again later. Besides, I had to get that box to the Candle Shoppe and prayed that Mr. Stilton wouldn't chew me out for being a little late, but as it turned out, being tardy was the least of my problems.

Chapter 6

I hurried over to the Candle Shoppe, while trying to remain under the speed limit and avoid getting a ticket. My mind reeled with thoughts about the circus, Cheryl, and the ringleader. I still didn't like the way he seemed unconcerned about how the tiger had gotten loose, which still hadn't been explained, and about Cheryl's death. When questioned, he had told Detective Shorts that he didn't feel emotions, such as fear, the way most people did, but that isn't what bothered me. There had been a look on his face when Cheryl died, as though he wasn't surprised, or knew more than he let on.

I pulled into the small parking area in the back of the Candle Shoppe. Of course, it was more of an alley with just enough space to squeeze a few cars in. I just wanted to get close enough to the back door so that I didn't have to lug that hefty box of specialty candlestick holders very far. I opened the door to get out of my car, but Al's demeanor at the circus still plagued me. I was already late so I decided that I could take a few minutes to see what I could find on him.

Reaching behind me seat, I pulled out my 2 in 1 laptop that I had stuffed under there after class a few days ago. I know what you're thinking, that it isn't smart to keep an electronic item like that in the car, but I wasn't too worried about it. My car had a good security system and it had Tiny's mark on the rear bumper, so most people stayed away from it. For those of you who don't know, Tiny is the leader of the local biker gang whom I had—and quite by accident—befriended. He had a reputation for being the sort of man you did not want to anger or steal from, but once he decided he liked you, he saw to it no one bothered you, which has proven helpful in my case.

I placed my 2 in 1 device in my lap and turned it on. Using my smartphone as a wifi hotspot, I pulled up the web browser and typed in "Al circus leader" Within moments the screen filled with articles about how circuses abuse animals, circuses are haunted (that one didn't surprise me), and the history of the circus. Okay. So I needed to narrow down my search. I decided to do a search about yesterday's events and typed in "woman dies at Vermont circus". Pay dirt. An image of Cheryl popped up with seven articles about her unfortunate death at the circus yesterday.

I checked my watch. It was well after 9 and I had to get inside. I was about to close the web browser when a headline at the bottom of the page caught my eye.

Performer Dies in Ohio Circus

I clicked on it. At the top of the page was a photo of a man that looked very similar to Al. Though an older photograph, the man possessed the same grim demeanor, stone-faced look, and hardened eyes. It was him. I skimmed the article even though it had the date of September 13, 2006.

Two days ago, the circus came to the little town of Dayton, Ohio. What should have been a joyous event filled with fun and spectacle for children and adults alike, turned to one of death. While on the high-rise, performing a stunt he had done for over 20 years, circus performer Jason Alderoy died, plummeting to his death in front of cheering onlookers. That cheering turned to frightened gasps when Mr. Alderoy fell.

Police are conducting an investigation, but thus far, authorities seem set on ruling it an accident. The cable that held the swing had snapped. According to investigators it appeared to have had a weak spot and when Mr. Alderoy placed his weight on it, that was enough to cause it to give way.

When asked about the tragedy, ringleader Al had nothing to say, except that this is the way life is in the circus, that sometimes accident happen. Though it isn't clear what his feelings about the

incident are, one thing is for certain Mr. Alderoy
will be missed by the other members of the circus.

I stared at the screen rereading the article. Al never told Detective Shorts about this incident. Though I
know that the two might not be connected, the fact that
this same circus, which Al has been with as ringleader, had suffered a similar accident did seem odd and the
question is: has it happened before?

I turned off the computer and called Jack.

"Mel, I really don't—"

"It's happened before," I interrupted him.

"What's happened before?"

"I found an article on the web that's about nine-
years-old. There was a circus in Ohio and a performer
died. It was ruled an accident, just like the way they are
ruling what happened yesterday as an accident."

"So?"

"Guess who was the ringleader of the circus in Ohio."

No response.

"Al."

"The same guy?"

"Yes. A bit odd isn't it?"

"It is interesting. I'll do some digging. See if I can
find anything more about our friend from the circus."

"Thanks."

My phone buzzed the moment I hung up with Jack. Jackie
had sent a text. I tapped the icon and the message popped up.

911. Get 2 the CS now!

911? I looked at the back door (CS was Jackie's abbreviation for the Candle Shoppe), knowing I would get an earful for how late I was, but what had Jackie so panicked? With no other choice, I opened the trunk to my car and reached in, heaving that box out and straining my back muscles with the effort. I plopped it on the edge of the trunk opening, balancing it as I prepared myself to walk the three yards from my car to the door with the ginormous box of stuff. At least now I knew why Mr. Stilton wanted someone else to get it. I grasped the sides of the box and used my knee to help lift it into my arms; a big huff of air escaped my mouth from the effort.

I pictured in my mind how I looked as I teetered from side to side, hurrying to the door before slamming the box into the brick wall next to it. While bracing myself against the box to hold it steady, and not drop it, I used my free hand to open the door before toppling inside. Somehow, and I'm not sure how, I managed to get that box to the table that was in the back room of the Candle Shoppe and dumped in on there with a loud bang.

"Mel, where have you been?" came Jackie's voice, but she spoke in a hushed whisper as though she didn't want to be overheard.

"Getting that thing." I pointed at the box. "Do you know how heavy it is?"

I noticed the panicked look on Jackie's face. Someone shifted in the background and as my eyes focused on the shadowed area, I realized it was Tammy pushing herself against the wall while wringing her hands together. "What is going on?" I demanded.

"It might be best if you look in there," replied Jackie, pointing at the door to Mr. Stilton's office.

Unsure of what I would find, and somewhat dreading it, I stalked up to the door, wrapped my clammy hand around the cool doorknob, and opened it. Inside, laying on Mr. Stilton's desk was Rocky the tiger. I slammed the door shut not believing what I had just seen. I opened the door again and poked my head in. Yep. It was the tiger. He looked up at me and rested his chin on his skillet pan-sized paws, filling the room with his roaring purr.

"What is he doing in there?" I asked.

Jackie turned her head towards Tammy.

That not only made sense, but explained everything as it was just the sort of thing Tammy would do.

"I couldn't just leave him there," wailed Tammy. "They were going to kill him!"

"So you brought him here!" I shouted, before covering my mouth, hoping that Mr. Stilton hadn't heard; but, as luck would have it, he did.

"Mel?" He walked into the backroom. "Mel, you are very late."

"I know," I replied, while both Jackie and Tammy stood in front of the door to his office, "but it took them half an hour to locate the box and you didn't warn me that it would be so heavy."

"A half hour to locate it?"

"Yes, and I know I should have called."

"And they didn't carry it out to your car for you?"

"No, I had to do that."

Mr. Stilton rubbed the stubble on his chin. "I'm going to have to talk to them about that. They always had someone put it in my car for me. I'm sorry about that, Mel. They're usually more organized down there. Uh… where is the box?"

I pointed at it.

Mr. Stilton walked over and opened it, pulling out some silver candlestick holders with gold and emerald mosaic carvings stretching up and down their stems. The bottom of the holder's flared out, forming a sort of bronze-colored flower.

"Those are exquisite," said Jackie, entranced by the delicate designs that dotted the rim on the top of the holders. "What are they for?"

"A couple came in weeks ago and ordered these for their wedding."

Jackie nudged me with her elbow, I guess to give me a hint of what Greg and I should do for our wedding, but we hadn't even set a date yet.

"Anyway," continued Mr. Stilton, "I'll put these aside. The couple should be in tomorrow to get them. Now, if you'll excuse me, I need to get something from my office."

"No!" Jackie, Tammy, and I all shouted at once.

Mr. Stilton glanced at each of us with a curious look on his face. "Is there something going on here that I should know about?"

"No!" the three of us answered in unison.

Mr. Stilton's eyebrows squished together in a doubtful expression and he crossed his arms, opening his mouth to speak when the table in the room scooted an inch. We all turned towards it. It moved a second time and a third.

"Oh, I hate it when my foot gets caught," said Cheryl.

She appeared from midair, forming a semisolid shape as the table continued to shift left and right from her efforts to untangle her foot from around one of its legs. When she noticed us all watching her, she squeaked and vanished, running into the main store and causing the table to jerk one more time.

Mr. Stilton stared after her, his mouth hanging open. "Did you—"

"No!" both Jackie and I said in unison.

A series of crashes sounded from the main area and Mr. Stilton ran off to see what had caused it. Jackie and I paused by the doorway, peering out as Cheryl's efforts to get away caused a cascade effect of items tumbling off shelves and landing at the feet of startled customers.

"We need to get that tiger out of here now," I said to her.

We both darted back to Mr. Stilton's office to find the door open and Tammy inside with the tiger.

"Who's a big and fluffy boy?" she cooed to it, rubbing its huge belly as the animal rolled on its back, purring up a storm. "You're just a sweetie, aren't you?"

"Do you think maybe he'll eat her?" Jackie asked as we watched in disbelief at the way Tammy burrowed herself into the tiger and at the way it enjoyed every minute of the attention.

"Not likely," I said.

"You're right. I don't think it ever left cub hood."

"Tammy," I hissed at her. "get over here."

Disappointed, Tammy pulled herself away from the tiger and came over. "I need you to go out there and help Mr. Stilton while Jackie and I take care of the tiger."

"But they'll kill him," protested Tammy.

"He can't stay here," I replied. "If they haven't noticed him missing by now, they will soon and we don't want him found here. Now, go!" I shoved Tammy through the room and into the main part of the shop.

"How did she get the tiger here in the first place?" I asked Jackie.

"You don't want to know," replied Jackie.

"I need you to get the door to the back seat open and think of a good excuse for why we need to take off for a little while. I'll get the tiger."

"A good excuse," said Jackie. "Right… uh… guess I'll think of something."

Jackie disappeared into the main part of the store before hurrying back and rushing out the back door to the alley. I have no idea what she said to Mr. Stilton, but Jackie was good at talking her way in and out of things.

I opened the door to Mr. Stilton's office. The tiger had jumped down to the floor and washed his front paw as I walked in, being careful not to startle him. He looked up and rolled over onto his side, lifting one paw at me while his tail waved back and forth. I knelt down, holding my left hand out to him. The tiger sniffed it with his wet nose and rubbed against it before bringing his paw up in a playful pat. While I stroked him with one hand, I used the other to grab the leash that was still attached to his collar.

"Come on, boy," I said, standing up and walking backwards to the door. "Come on."

The tiger just rolled back over, ignoring me. Typical cat, even if he was a big cat. Frustrated, I marched over to

Mr. Stilton's desk—he usually kept his lunch in there—and pulled out a brown paper bag with a ham sandwich in it. I hoped the tiger liked ham as I pulled out the sandwich and unwrapped it.

"Are you hungry?" I said to it.

The tiger's head jerked up and it licked his chops.

"Come this way if you want the sandwich."

The animal rolled onto its stomach, getting to its feet. I continued to walk backwards, keeping one hand clasped to the leash, while my other hand held the ham sandwich out, urging the tiger to follow me. With my foot, I kicked the exit door open and pushed my way out. Jackie stood by my car with the rear door open, her nervous movements almost eradicating my calm demeanor. I tossed the sandwich into the backseat of my car and the tiger jumped in after. Once it had laid down, I grabbed the sleeping bags I kept in the trunk of my car and threw it over the tiger, covering it.

"Now what?" asked Jackie.

"Now," I replied, "we go to Tiny's."

"Tiny's?"

"Yeah. We'll need a distraction in order to sneak the tiger back into its cage and Tiny and his gang are really good at that."

We both took one last look at the covered mound in the backseat before getting into the car and driving off while being serenaded by the tiger's constant purring.

I pulled out my phone and dialed Tiny.

"Yo," he said on the first ring.

"Tiny, it's Mel. I need a favor."

"Another one?"

"Yeah. I have a bit of a problem in the backseat of my car."

"How big of a problem?"

"Oh, I'd say about eight feet in length and 200 pounds."

"I'll send one of my boys over and—"

"I'm bringing it to you."

"To me?"

"Yep. I'll be there in five minutes."

I hung up. I knew I had asked Tiny to help me out a lot the last few years and this just might be a bit more than he wanted to handle; I just hoped he'd be willing to. I pulled into the garage where he and his friends worked. Tiny had an apartment above it.

"Mel," said Tiny, walking up to me as I got out of my car, "what's this 200-pound problem you have?"

I rolled down the window to the backseat and pulled up the sleeping bag to reveal the tiger underneath.

"Are you kidding me?" He and his gang all jumped back in surprise. "Don't tell me that you kidnapped that tiger from the circus."

"I didn't," I replied. "Tammy did. I need your help to get him back."

"How can we help?" Tiny asked, staring at the tiger while it rested its head on its front paws and stared back at him with soulful eyes.

"Jackie and I plan to sneak him back into the compound, but what we need a distraction."

"Which is where I come in," said Tiny.

I smiled in response.

"All right boys," said Tiny to everyone around us, "we're going to the circus."

"One other thing," I said to him, "do you still have that big steak of yours?"

Tiny glared at me.

"I'll pay you back."

He jerked his head in the direction of the steps that led to his apartment, thus giving me his permission. Thanking him, I hiked up the stairs and went inside his little studio apartment, going straight to the refrigerator and where the 64-ounce steak he had was. I found a plastic bag and stuck the chunk of meat in it before running back outside and to the parking lot below, making a mental note to buy Tiny a new steak.

When I arrived back at the car, Jackie was dancing from foot to foot in an anxious fervor. "Can we go now?"

I nodded, placing the steak in the trunk, recovering the tiger with the sleeping bag, and getting in the car. The trip seemed to take longer than I remembered from the previous times I had gone to the circus, but I didn't have a tiger in the back of my car then.

"Quit fidgeting," I said to Jackie as she wrung her hands for the 20th time.

"I can't," she replied, glancing back at the still mound in the backseat. "I usually prefer to have a set of bars between me and giant predators."

I checked my rear view mirror, peering at the sleeping bag as it shifted and a soft purr emanated from it. "Somehow, I get the feeling that he's not much of a predator."

Jackie glared at me.

"Don't worry," I reassured her. "We'll get him back where he belongs."

"Until Tammy decides to break him out again," mumbled Jackie.

I snorted. What was that girl thinking? I pulled onto a dirt road that lead up to a small wooded area that bordered a remote edge of the circus. After I had parked behind some foliage, Tiny and his gang roared past, heading straight for the entrance.

"Now what?" asked Jackie.

"Now, we wait."

I watched from my vantage point as Tiny and his boys rode up to the entrance, making as much noise as they could, shouting insults at one another and laughing in a cantankerous manner.

The man at the entrance ran up to them. "You all need to leave."

"Aw, come on man," said Tiny, "we want to see the circus. Right, boys?"

Shouts of agreement went up.

"The circus is closed for the moment," said the man at the gate.

While Tiny and his gang booed and shouted insults at the poor man, I went back to Jackie. "We don't have much time," I told her.

I went to the trunk and opened it, getting the raw steak out while Jackie opened the back door to my car. "Come on, boy," I said, waving the chunk of meat in front of me.

The tiger's ears perked up and he lifted his head, licking his lips and a part of me wondered if he thought I was lunch instead of the steak. I waved the meat some more. The tiger jumped out of the car while Jackie stood frozen to the ground, unable to move and too afraid that the animal might turn on her.

"Come on," I called to the tiger, leading him closer to the secluded area of the circus. I didn't know how I was going to get him back in his bunker without being noticed, but it seemed that luck was on my side, for at that moment, I heard Ramone's voice.

"Rocky!" he called.

I froze. I hadn't counted on the trainer looking for the tiger, though I wasn't surprised that he had noticed the animal missing.

"Rocky!"

"I still can't believe he named the tiger that," Jackie whispered as she came up beside me.

"Ramone!" Al walked up to him and I crouched, clutching the meat while the tiger kept nudging against my hand, pulling at it in an effort to get it away from me. I pushed him aside and he just rolled over onto his back, batting at my hand.

"Look, Ramone," said Al, "the tiger isn't anywhere. We can't keep the fact that he is missing a secret for much longer."

"He's got to be around here somewhere. What if someone else finds him. What if…"

"Let's keep looking a little bit longer," said Al.

"Somehow, I don't think we'll be able to get the tiger back in his cage unnoticed," said Jackie.

"Maybe not," I replied. "How far can you throw?"

"Not very."

Whistles permeated the air and I knew that Tiny and

his friends were running out of ideas to distract the guy at the gate. With nothing left to lose, I wriggled the meat in front of the tiger, who followed it with uneven jerks of his head, raised my arm up, and chucked it over the bushes I had hidden behind and into the field beyond. The tiger leapt over the brush, almost knocking Jackie and me over, and pounced on the steak, devouring it.

"Rocky!" yelled an ecstatic Ramone as he ran up to the tiger. The animal hunkered into the grass, gnawing on its piece of meat while Ramone petted him, pleased to have found him.

Al walked up with a perplexed look on his face. "Where did that hunk of meat come from?"

Ramone didn't answer.

I tapped Jackie's arm and motioned for her to follow me deeper into the trees. We had just hidden behind two tall oaks when Ramone's face appeared above the bushes we had been hiding behind moments before. His eyes roamed the area, while my heart pounded my ribcage, and for a moment, I thought it might burst free, like in that movie *Alien*. Craning my neck, I peeked around the chipped bark of the tree trunk, relieved when I saw Al's back disappearing into the distance. The thunderous roar of a bunch of motorcycles raced past, drowning the cheery chirps of the birds that flittered from branch to branch above us.

"What's that?" I heard Ramone's distant voice.

"Who knows?" replied Al as he and the trainer took the tiger back to where the animal belonged.

I breathed a sigh of relief and looked at Jackie and her

calmed face said it all. I heard a branch snap. Something told me that we were not alone out there so I walked towards the sound, ignoring Jackie's protests. Just over a small rise, I saw a woman. "Excuse me," I called to her.

She turned around and ran off frightened.

"We don't…"

The woman had disappeared.

"What was that all about?" asked Jackie.

"I don't know, but I would have liked to have talked to her."

"I hear that circus folk are a tightknit group. They'll only talk to their own kind. They don't like outsiders."

I frowned. We both hurried back to my car and high-tailed it out of there, not wanting to get caught and we had to get back to work. I had no idea what kind of chaos Cheryl had caused at the Candle Shoppe. I just hoped it wasn't more than we could handle.

Chapter 7

I tossed and turned, unable to sleep, which seemed to be the new habit around here, especially when I had a mystery on my mind. I glanced at my clock and frowned when it told me that it was one in the morning. Drinking glasses tinkled in the kitchen and I had a feeling of who had stopped by for a visit. I threw off my blanket and tiptoed down the hallway to the kitchen.

SMASH!

I cringed, not wanting to know what Cheryl had knocked over this time. Jackie's door opened and she shuffled out, rubbing the sleep from her eyes. "Please tell me that we don't have a guest," she said.

I didn't say anything and walked into the kitchen where I found Cheryl trying to pick up a cast iron skillet, but it kept slipping, literally, through her fingers. I reached down and picked it up. "It's late," I said to her.

Cheryl looked up at me with tearful eyes. Did ghosts cry? Her bottom lip quivered and I knew that at any moment she would break down.

"I'm not upset," I said to her, hoping to calm her down before she started sobbing.

"It's not the pan," wailed Cheryl. "It's everything! I shouldn't be dead! I'm too young." She faded in an out with each word until she settled on a semitransparent form.

Not knowing what else to do, I led her to a chair and helped her sit down, though I could see the impression in the furniture as she settled in. Jackie sat across from her, knowing that she would not be getting any sleep tonight, and I think she was just as curious as I was about why Cheryl had shown up.

"Why don't you start at the beginning," I said, grabbing a box of tissue before rethinking my decision. Ghosts couldn't shed real tears, or maybe they could as I watched an ethereal tear mosey down Cheryl's see-through cheek. I snatched the box of tissues again and held it out to her and she took one.

"I don't want to be here," said Cheryl.

"What do you mean?" I asked as Jackie leaned in closer.

"I had dreams. Things I wanted to do."

Here it comes. The realization that she was murdered had sunk in. Some ghosts handled it well, like Rachel who just vowed to get revenge, and others didn't.

"I thought if my death was an accident, then I could handle it, but today at the mortuary, it became all too apparent that it wasn't."

"I'm sorry," I said, patting her hand, though mine just went right through it. "We'll find the person who did this. I promise."

Jackie nodded in agreement.

"What we need to do is talk to the people at the circus again," I said, "without the police around."

"That's going to be difficult," replied Cheryl.

"Why's that?" asked Jackie.

"Circus people don't really like strangers," said Cheryl. "You have to be one of them."

"We could pretend to join for a day," said Jackie.

Cheryl shook her head. "They don't just take you for a day. Though, they do hire locals to help with setting up and cleaning. Sometimes the owner hires locals to be part of some of the acts, mostly the clown ones. It helps bring in bigger crowds. People seem to love watching their friends get doused with a firehose."

I had an idea, and I knew Jackie and Greg would both hate it, but it might be the only way to get some information. I grabbed my phone and dialed Greg, hoping he wouldn't be too angry at me for waking him up.

"MMPH," came his groggy voice over the phone.

"Greg?"

"Mel, it's one in the morning."

"I know, but Chery is here and…"

"I'll be right over."

Within two minutes he walked through the door.

"Morning!" said Cheryl, trying to be cheerful, swinging her hand as she spoke and knocking a vase off the table next to her. "I'm sorry."

"Don't worry about it," I said, picking it up as water spilled from the top.

"So"—Greg stifled a yawn—"what's the emergency?"

"Mel wants to go to the circus, in disguise," replied Jackie.

He looked at me. "That's a new one."

"I need to talk to the people there. See if they noticed something unusual, or maybe they can give me a hint as to who might have wanted to harm Cheryl." I didn't mention that I had Al as my primary suspect.

"Well, I always wanted to perform at the circus," joked Greg.

"Oh, they won't take you," said Cheryl. "Oh—I didn't—it's just you don't—oh, I've put my foot in it."

"Could he be a helping hand?" asked Jackie.

"Yeah!" Cheryl's face lit up. "You could work in the background as one of the people who help set up. Al and the owner is always hiring locals to do that and you get paid."

"Works for me," said Greg.

"The owner or Al might hire you two to be in one of the acts," said Cheryl, pointing at Jackie and me.

"Then, it's settled," said Greg. "We'll go tomorrow. Poke around and see if we can learn anything." He laid his head on the arm of the couch and drifted off to sleep while I grabbed a blanket and wrapped it over him.

"I think we ought to go to bed," I said as Greg snored and I wished that I could fall asleep that fast.

Jackie and I headed to our rooms, leaving Greg on the couch and Cheryl in the chair. She assured me that she would be fine, but a part of me wondered how much of that was true, or just her trying to ease my worrying about her.

The next morning, I woke up early, right at sunrise, and tiptoed to the kitchen to start the coffee, setting out the creamers and sweeteners that we each liked to use. Greg groaned as he turned over, the belt of his robe hung over the edge of the couch in oval loops. He snorted when he turned and I smiled, wondering how I would deal with his snoring once we were married. Guess I was going to have to look into those breathing strips.

Jackie moseyed into the kitchen with a huge yawn, her hair falling in waves around her face. I swear she brushed right after waking up, but she always swore that it was always that perfect. I didn't know how she did it.

"I can see why you haven't moved in together, yet. Does he always snore like that?"

"Most nights." I handed her a fresh cup of coffee. "Of course I have another reason for not moving in with him yet."

"HMMM. What?"

"Aunt Ethel."

Jackie slammed her coffee cup on the counter and charged me, snatching the collar of my shirt in her hands and stared at me with a crazed look in her eyes. "Please tell me she isn't here. My sanity can't take it. I'm not giving up my privacy again for that crazy old—"

"She's not here."

"Oh." Jackie let go of my shirt and smoothed it out where her grip had crumpled it. "Don't scare me like that. You know your aunt is—"

"Insane?"

"More like bat you-know-what crazy."

"Who's crazy?" asked Greg, scratching his ruffled hair as he shuffled into the kitchen.

"Her aunt," replied Jackie.

"She's not..." began Greg.

"She's not here."

Relief filled his face. He must have been thinking the same dark scenarios that Jackie always envisioned whenever the discussion of my aunt came up.

"Here," I said, handing him a cup of coffee with half and half and that new Zevia sweetener.

He took it and drained it in one gulp, complete with sound effects.

As I reached for the pot of coffee, the coffee maker shot out from the wall, leaving marks on the counter, and crashed on the floor. Hot brown liquid spread everywhere and some of it had splattered on the white doors of the lower cabinets. Cheryl materialized, but still remained translucent. Her hand hang above the counter and an apologetic expression crossed her face as she looked at us. "Sorry."

"How did you survive 20 years of life?" asked Jackie. I think her statement just came out before she had a chance to reconsider it.

Cheryl hung her head.

"It's okay," I comforted her, trying to pat her shoulder, but it went right through her and made my hand feel clammy. "We were thinking of replacing it anyway, maybe with one of those new Keurigs."

She managed a weak smile.

"We need to get going," I said, glancing at my watch and realizing that we had wasted an hour just socializing.

Jackie ran to her room, where I heard her closet doors slam and bang as she chose the right outfit and Greg rushed to his apartment across the hall, coming out of it a minute later all dressed. We took Jackie's car in order to share on the cost of gas, and she insisted on driving for a change, arriving at the circus just as people were setting up for the next show.

"They really don't take time off, do they?" asked Jackie as she parked the car in what looked to be a good spot.

"Can't," whispered Cheryl.

I jumped a bit. I never even knew that she had gotten in the car with us.

"What if Al catches us?" I asked, thinking about it all of the sudden. He did know us and he had caught me when I had snooped around the first time.

The blank looks on Jackie's and Greg's faces told me that they hadn't thought of that either.

"Don't go to him," said Cheryl.

"But isn't he…" began Greg.

"No," interrupted Cheryl, "he is only the ringleader. Runs the shows, but he is not the owner. That is who you have to speak to. Oh, but I have an even better idea."

Cheryl disappeared. We glanced at one another, wondering what she was up to when a pile of red and yellow polka-dotted clothes struck the window, followed by two pairs of duck-shaped shoes.

"What is all this?" I asked, stepping out of the car.

"Sorry about that," replied Cheryl. "I meant to just hand them to you, but… oh, you know."

"But what are we to do with them?"

"Put them on!" Cheryl looked around before lowering her voice. "The first show starts in about ten minutes and it's the clown show. Everyone is in that tent there getting ready. Two of you can put these on and pretend to be one of them while you talk to them."

I had to hand it to her. That was good thinking. Jackie and I put the clown outfits on over our clothes, tying our hair up in buns with a pack of hair ties that Jackie always kept in the glove compartment of her car. Before we had a chance to sneak over to the tent, a man dressed in a yellow jumpsuit with green and pink strips all over it stormed up to us.

"Hey!" His white-painted face made his harsh tone even more frightening and I was certain that we would get kicked off the premises, but as luck would have it, he thought we were supposed to be there. "What are you two doing out here?"

Jackie and I looked at one another and I noticed that Greg had disappeared along with Cheryl.

"Uh…" I started, but didn't know what to say.

"Get in there! We're on in ten minutes and you two don't have your makeup on!"

Jackie and I ran off to the tent not wanting to argue, and glad that he didn't think we were up to anything suspicious. We burst into the tent and the bustle of activity that lay inside as more clowns, acrobats, and other performers scurried about in an effort to be ready on time. I couldn't believe the amount of bright lights in there from all of the vanity mirrors so that people could put on their make-up.

"What are you two standing around for?" demanded a female clown, the ire in her eyes unnerved me. "Find a mirror and some face paint. Come on! We don't have much time."

"They don't waste much time mourning their own, do they?" Jackie whispered in my ear.

"One of the perils of working in a circus," Cheryl whispered back as Jackie and I painted our faces with the shimmering white face paint. "And I wasn't the most popular person here." She swung her hand, causing a tray of cosmetics to topple over.

"Be careful with that!" barked a woman next to me, wearing a tight spandex outfit; its neon pink almost hurt my eyes.

"Sorry," I said. "It was an accident."

She rolled her eyes at me, releasing an exasperated sigh before stalking off, muttering something about newbies.

"Don't worry about her," said another woman, about Cheryl's age, as she picked up the tray.

I continued to stare at her, wondering where I had seen her before, and it hit me: she was the woman that Jackie and I had surprised in the woods when we returned the tiger.

The woman placed the tray with its contents on a nearby table.

"Sorry," I said when I realized that I had been staring at her. "You just look familiar."

"No worries."

"I hear that there was an accident a couple of days

ago," I said, diving right into it and hoping not to scare the girl away again.

"Yeah," she replied.

"Sorry. I didn't mean to..."

"It's okay. Her name was Cheryl." The saddened tone in her voice filled the empty space between us.

"Were you two close?"

"Like sisters. She had run away from home. I always told her she'd have to go back and face her parents someday, but I guess someday never came. I'm Ellie, by the way."

"Mel."

Ellie grabbed some red blush and applied it to my cheeks in huge circles, finishing the clown look. "You don't normally do this sort of work, do you?" she asked.

"How can you tell?"

"Because you put your face paint on before applying the cream."

She pointed at a container of facial cream and I reached for it, but before I could grab it, Cheryl decided to try and hand it to me. The cream flew from the vanity, crashing into a mirror—I hoped she didn't believe in that seven years' bad luck superstition—and plopped on the floor amidst a pile of razor-sharp shards of glass. People turned and glared at me. "Oops," I said, shrugging my shoulders.

They shook their heads and went back to putting their own make-up on while Ellie laughed. "That's what Cheryl always did."

"What?" I asked, not believing that my mishap opened the gates to her talking.

"The girl who died, her name was Cheryl. She was such a klutz. Always knocking things over."

Tears welled up in her eyes and I placed a comforting hand on her shoulder.

"It never should have happened," continued Ellie.

"What do you mean?"

"Cheryl was upset that morning. I don't know why. When I asked her about it, all she said was that she had overheard something between Al and the owner."

"Ellie, you shouldn't spread rumors," said an older woman, approaching us.

"I'm not," Ellie retorted.

"Rumors?" I asked, hoping to glean some more information.

"Well, everyone knows that this circus is in a bit of financial trouble, but the rumor is that the owner wants to sell. There's no way he would do such a thing. It would put all of us out of a job."

"Come on, everyone! Get out there now!" screamed an angry voice.

The clowns rushed from the tent and to the one next to it where Al stood in the ring, making his huge announcement about the next show. As people hurried about, I picked up the container of cream and opened it, sniffing the contents. It had no smell, but the smooth texture gave every indication that it was your standard facial cream.

"That's not mine," whispered Cheryl.

I looked at her, confused.

"Everyone has their own container for hygiene purposes. That one isn't mine."

Angry shouts caught my attention and I turned away from Cheryl, placing the facial cream on a table before creeping to the side of the tent and crouching next to it, doing my best to not lose my balance.

"You know I can't do that!" said a gruff, male voice in a hushed tone as though he didn't want anyone to hear him.

I inched closer.

"You said you would pay me $100,000!"

Pay him? I strained to listen to every word, forgetting where I was and that I had to get out of there, but was more interested in learning about what the $100,000 was for.

"I can't keep this circus going any longer. It's losing money. You know that."

The man shifted closer and the dancing shadow on the tent wall told me the he was talking on a cell phone.

"No, he's okay with it.... He has to be. Al may run the shows, but I am the one who owns this circus."

I shifted a bit to get a more comfortable position.

"Of course he's not happy, but..."

"Come on!" A man seized my arm, forcing me to my feet, and shoved me out the tent and into the one where the other clowns were doing their performance. I spotted Jackie in an instant and realized that she had gotten dragged out there as well.

The roar of the crowds failed to drown my pulse as it thundered in my ear and throbbed in my neck. My eyes must have turned into saucers as I scanned the laughing and bobbing people in the bleachers, though in the front sat four with their arms crossed and sour looks on their faces and... Tammy? What was she doing here?

"Hey!" said an irritated voice.

I turned and one of the clowns snatched my shoulders and shoved me towards the others as they pretended to have a dance off.

"Get in your proper position!" he hissed in my ear.

I crashed into three of the other clowns, knocking them into the sand before landing in it face first. They cursed me before jumping back to their feet and going into their next act. Glancing up, I watched as Jackie mimicked their movements with ease, smiling wide. She either enjoyed it, or was good at putting on a performance, something I wished I could do as tufts of sand were kicked up in my face. I rose to my knees and before I had a chance to knock some sand out of areas that should always remain clear of the gritty stuff, hands seized my arms, hauling me to my feet and pushing me into the circle of dancing clowns. The dizzying music did not help my equilibrium as I was turned, twisted, pushed, and shoved in every direction.

Drums sounded and the clowns stopped as a trampoline was rolled out. Silence followed. Unease filled me and I looked up to see what they stared at and almost fainted. A ladder led up to what looked like a diving board and I watched as one person climbed it, spread his arms out, and jumped, bouncing off the trampoline and into the arms of the clowns waiting on the other side. My heart leapt into my throat and I had to swallow hard to get the lump out of there. I looked at Jackie. Her eyes were as wide as mine and almost popped out of her head as others pushed her to the ladder and forced her to go up.

Sweat dripped down my neck as I watched. I tried closing my eyes, but curiosity always took over. Jackie stepped onto the board and looked around before swan diving off, doing a flip, and landing on the trampoline. She flew off, mimicking a bird, and into the waiting arms of the other clowns. The breath that I had been holding eased out of my mouth as relief washed over me.

Hands seized my arms again.

"What? No!" I said to the person they belonged to.

He didn't listen as he shoved me to the ladder and forced me up it. I tried to back away, but more hands pushed me upward. Once at the top, I surveyed the crowd, my hands shaking from nerves as I inched my way to the edge of the board, wondering what I was to do.

"Hurry up!" yelled one of the clowns waiting to catch me.

My breathing quickened and my feet refused to budge.

"You have to tuck and roll," Cheryl whispered in my ear, appearing by my side.

"What?" I said, having difficulty hearing her over the overexcited crowd.

"You have to tuck and..." Cheryl moved closer to show me what to do, but her movements knocked me off balance and I fell over the side.

My heart jumped again as I free-fell. A stinging pain struck my back when I hit the trampoline and sunk into it as it molded around me before springing upward and propelling me into the air. I watched in horror as I sailed over the other bemused clowns—I spotted Jackie's terrified face amongst the sea of red noses and white paint—and saw the pile of crates approaching fast. I smashed into them, though lucky for me, they were made of Styrofoam and weren't real. My head spun. I tried shifting underneath the pile of painted Styrofoam, but my body hurt too much. Stomping feet, followed by ice being shaken in a cup, rushed up to me.

"That was awesome!" shouted a familiar voice. My foggy brain tried to put the voice with the face I knew it had to belong to just as a chunk of Styrofoam was lifted off me. "Mel?"

Tammy. I turned my head and looked up at her, still dazed.

"I don't think that clown is very funny," said a bored man from the stands.

"Oh, shut up!" Tammy shouted back, flinging her soda cup at him. It struck him in the face and the top popped off, covering the man in cola.

I shifted my legs as I tried to stand up, but Tammy grabbed one of my arms, while Jackie ran up and seized my other one, and pulled me to my feet.

"We need to find Greg and get out of here," I said. I swung my head around and spotted Al, whose sharp gaze made me uneasy. Did he recognize us? We all ran through the arena, ramming our way through the other clowns, hoping to get out of there.

"Over here!" I heard Cheryl yell and pointed in her direction, urging them to go to her.

She jumped up and down, waving at me, but stumbled and toppled over, tripping one of the clowns as he ran across the ring, which caused him to fall over and trip another clown, thus starting a domino effect. Tammy, Jackie, and I ran past them, jumping over anyone laying on the ground and squeaked through the opening that Cheryl had pointed us to.

A whistle caught my attention. Greg waved us over. We ran to him, stripping off our clown attire as we went and wiping the makeup off our faces.

"I think you missed some right there," Tammy said to Jackie, pointing at a spot behind her ear.

Jackie smacked her hand away.

"What are you doing here?" I asked Tammy, thinking she was supposed to be at work.

"I took an extended lunch break and came back here," she said. "I thought I could do some sleuthing."

"What did you find?" I asked.

"The owner wants to sell the circus," replied Tammy.

I tried to keep my face interested since I didn't want to reveal that I already had learned that bit of news. "Anything else?"

"Well, he and that Al guy had a bit of an argument over it. I overheard them having another one. It wasn't too difficult to guess that they had been at it before."

Jackie gave me a look of surprise. I guess she didn't think that Tammy had it in her to do some real detective work.

"Hey!"

We turned around. An irate Al marched straight for us, waving his switch in sharp jerks. Before he could get any closer, two police cars pulled up and parked in front of him, forcing him to stop. Out stepped Detective Shorts. I grabbed Greg and the others and pulled them into the shadows, hoping that the detective hadn't noticed us. I didn't need another lecture from him.

"Al Swanson?"

"Yeah?"

"I need to ask you to come down to the station."

"Ask me?" Al glanced at the other officers. "Looks more like you're telling me."

"It's up to you if you want to make a scene or not."

Al flung his switch into the dirt and allowed an officer to place him in the back of a police cruiser. We watched as the detective got in a car and they two vehicles pulled away.

"We should go see the tiger," said Tammy after Detective Shorts left.

"Uh, no," said Jackie. "We need to leave."

I agreed with her and had a suspicion that the tiger was Tammy's real reason for being at the circus in the first place. "Tammy, isn't your lunch break almost over?"

"Oh no!" Tammy skedaddled out of there, running past tents and tables to the parking area.

I looked around for Cheryl, but didn't see her. Not wanting to stick around, I motioned for us to leave, saying, "We should go too."

Chapter 8

The next morning, I went to work with little fanfare. I still hadn't seen Cheryl since Al had been taken into custody by Detective Shorts. Where had she gone? Had she finally found some peace? I hoped she had. Poor girl.

I walked through the back door of the office and into the back room where the lockers for our things were as well as any extra supplies. Jackie didn't have to be in today, but I knew I would be working with Tammy. Though Al seemed like a likely candidate to have murdered Cheryl, and he did have a criminal record, something didn't add up. He and the owner seemed to have been having constant arguments, but where did Cheryl fit in? I was still no closer to knowing what had actually caused her death.

My eyes rested on the door to Mr. Stilton's office. It

was closed like it always was, but I found myself wondering if the tiger was back in there. I wouldn't have put it past Tammy to do such a thing. After hanging up my jacket, I stalked over to the door, paused, and listened just outside it. I didn't hear anything. I opened the door a crack and peeked in. It was empty. Breathing a sigh of relief, I closed it and turned around only to be greeted by Tammy's exuberant face.

"Morning!" she said in a cheery voice.

I always wondered how she managed to be so cheerful all the time. "Morning," I replied.

"What were you doing in Mr. Stilton's office?"

"Just making certain that there weren't any unwanted surprises."

I brushed past her and headed to the main area of the store where even this early in the morning people were shopping. As she followed after me, some sunlight that came in from the main window hit Tammy's arm and that was when I noticed some red marks on it.

"What happened to your arm?" I asked.

Tammy glanced at her arm and smiled. "Just hives."

"Just hives? Do you have allergies?" I was a bit worried about the possibility of her having an allergic reaction to something. It had never occurred to me that she could have allergies.

"It's nothing," Tammy said, waving away my concern. "I have a slight nut allergy. Last night I bought some crackers, but didn't read the label about whether it was made in a factory that contained nuts. Normally, it's not a problem, but I guess this time it was."

"Shouldn't you, maybe, go to a doctor?" I have heard

of people who were allergic to a particular food having a severe reaction of they ever consumed it.

"I'm fine. My allergy to nuts isn't that bad. The most that ever happens is that I break out in hives for a day, so I take some over the counter stuff and I'm usually good to go. The worst part is just the itchiness of the hives themselves."

"You're sure?" I glanced at a couple who had walked in and perused the shelves with vague looks of mild interest.

"Yep. You won't be rid of me that easily."

Good to know, though I kept that part to myself.

"Now, my cousin, though, he has a severe allergy to shellfish."

"What?" I faced her again, my interest piqued.

"Yeah," continued Tammy, "he can't even be around it without getting nauseous and if he gets just a little bit of it on his skin, he could risk anaphylactic shock."

"Really?" I had heard of people having a severe reaction to nuts, but shellfish? An idea hit me. What if Cheryl was allergic to something?

"So," I said to Tammy, "if I wanted to murder your cousin, hypothetically, all I would have to do is find a way to touch him with shellfish?"

"Basically," replied Tammy." Hey, you're not thinking of—"

"Tammy, you're a genius!" I hugged her and ran off to a small corner of the store where I could pull out my phone and call Jack, leaving a very bewildered Tammy alone next to the display of wax warmers.

"What now, Mel?" Jack answered his phone in a bored tone.

"Is it possible that if someone died from an allergic reaction to something, that it would not come up in the coroner's report?"

"Maybe," said Jack. "What have you found out?"

"So nothing would come up in the toxicology report?"

"Not likely. And about that report, Detective Shorts had the medical examiner rerun some test. They only thing that came up was some derivative of soy was found on her skin and her bloodwork showed that she had experienced an allergic reaction to something."

"So then she died of a severe allergic reaction?"

"It's possible. The medical examiner still hasn't made the ruling official."

"What?"

"She's afraid of losing her job," Jack said. "She's new. Hired a few months ago. The old ME had been around for over 40 years and had a lot seniority. He could get away with telling people where to shove it and would have done his job the right way, but no one would have dared fired him. But his hands started shaking too much when he performed autopsies so the city had to retire him."

"So why would the new ME not run the proper tests?" I asked, as I looked around to make sure Mr. Stilton didn't catch me on the phone.

"The politics of the situation. As I've said before, the police commissioner and the mayor want this wrapped up. It's easier to pin it on a tiger than try and prove that it was murder. And who uses a tiger to commit murder anyway?"

"Someone did," I said. "When I was there the day

Cheryl died, she acted disoriented. Like she was dizzy. Is that normal in an allergic reaction. Besides, I don't think she even ate anything.

"I don't know. I don't have a medical degree and—Wait! I'll just get the ME on the phone. Keep quiet though, because I'm going to do a three-way call."

I covered the mouthpiece of my phone as the couple that had walked in minutes before left with nothing. I heard Jack dial the number and the phone ring before someone picked up.

"Hello?"

"Miss Evanick?" said Jack.

"Yes."

"It's Jack from the IT department. I have a question and I was wondering if you could answer it."

"All right, I have a few minutes."

"I'm just wondering, is it possible to react to something just by getting it on your skin?"

"Look, I'm already getting enough grief from the detective about this—"

"I have an allergy to peanuts," Jacki lied; I knew that he had no such allergy, "and someone spilled some peanut oil at home this morning and some of it got on my skin. The reason for asking is I don't want to have to go to the hospital if it's nothing, but the area is all red and seems to be developing a rash."

"It's possible that your allergy can also result in a skin reaction," said the medical examiner. She must have bought Jack's story and nut allergies were common.

"Is being a bit dizzy part of that?"

"You feel light-headed?" The concern in the woman's voice came through.

"A little bit. It started soon after the oil touched my skin."

"People react differently to things. The most common reactions are hives and perhaps dizziness. In more severe cases the person's throat can swell up and they can go into anaphylactic shock. Do you have an epi pen?"

"It expired. I need to get a new one."

"Better do so."

"Is it possible to vomit from a food allergy? I'm feeling a little nauseous as well."

"Some reactions can result in severe vomiting and diarrhea. I knew someone who was allergic to chocolate. She never broke out in hives, but after an hour of eating anything with cocoa in it, she would vomit."

"And all this could happen just from touching peanut oil?"

"If your allergy is severe enough, yes, even topical application can trigger a response. Some people with severe nut allergies are known to break out in hives when they smell peanuts. Are you sure you're okay? Should I send someone to check on you?"

"I think I'll be fine. I'm going to take off early and someone is bringing me some over the counter medication for the rash."

"Well, you take it easy and if you start having difficulty breathing, get to the emergency room ASAP."

"Will do. Thanks."

The moment Jack hung up on Miss Evanick a stern voice, which I recognized right away, came through. "Your arm looks fine to me."

I imagined Jack's embarrassment as he realized that Detective Shorts had been listening to the entire conversation.

"Who's on the phone?" demanded the detective.

I cringed as I listened, knowing that I would be found out.

"No one," said Jack.

"Then why is the call is still connected?"

Scuffling noises came through the earpiece and I assumed that Jack had handed his phone to Detective Shorts.

"Miss Summers, I know this is you."

Yep. He figured it out all right. So, I did a stupid thing and pretended that he had the wrong number, even though I knew he could just look at Jack's list of recent calls.

"Uh, there's no one here by that name." I pressed the end button. That could not have gone any worse even if I had tried.

My phone buzzed. I didn't have to look at the caller ID to know that it was Detective Shorts calling. I hit the ignore button. Within seconds my phone buzzed again. Knowing I was not going to get out of this, I accepted the call.

"Miss Summers?"

"Yes," my voice squeaked.

"In the future, try be stealthier when prying information from Jack."

I cursed under my breath.

"And you are not to go to the circus alone in an effort to snoop around."

"But..."

"I mean it. Stay away from there."

"Yes, detective."

He hung up. A second later my phone buzzed and I received a text from Jack.

> *Meant to tell you. They let Al go.*
> *Didn't have enough to hold him.*

What? Why didn't that surprise me? I needed to talk to Cheryl, but where was she?

In answer to my question, a shelf with books about candle making fell over, sending the line of paperbacks toppling to the floor. I watched as the books tried to pick themselves up, but with each one that managed to hover in the air, two more from another shelf fell. Before any of the customers noticed the books that tried to put themselves back on the shelf, I ran over to it, resetting the shelf and picked up the books.

"Cheryl?" I whispered.

"I didn't realize this was here," she said.

"Keep your voice down." I looked around at some of the odd glances coming my way. "Where were you?"

"I felt bad after what had happened yesterday. If it wasn't for my idea, you wouldn't have almost gotten hurt."

"Don't worry about it." I looked around some more. Tammy busied herself with arranging the candle warmers into a pyramid—and I could just see that coming crashing down—while the few customers in the store ignored me. There was no sign of Mr. Stilton.

"Cheryl," I continued in a low voice, "are you allergic to anything."

"Soy."

I looked at her.

"I'm very allergic to soy. Can't even have it touch my skin."

"How bad is it?"

"Once, I ingested some as a child and my parents had to rush me to the emergency room because I couldn't breathe."

"So if you were to get some on your skin…"

"I guess I could react to it, but I've been very careful. I've had to go to an all organic diet because soy is in everything in various forms. I couldn't even eat pizza, unless I made it myself."

"Really?"

"Yeah, it's in the dough of most commercially made pizzas."

I felt bad for her. I had pizza on a weekly basis and here she was unable to touch it. I reached for one of the books, but it was just far enough away where I couldn't touch it.

"I'll get that." Cheryl rushed to the book, but her foot somehow had gotten caught on the floor rug we had and she tripped, bumping into a man who was on his way out the door. "Sorry," Cheryl said to him, and his eyes widened in fright, He wasn't able to see her and it must have seemed that the air was apologizing to him.

"He left in a hurry," commented Cheryl as the man rushed out the door and hurried down the sidewalk.

I didn't say anything, not wanting to hurt her feelings by reminding her that she was a ghost and not everyone is used to such things.

"Are you also allergic to coconuts?" I asked her.

"Oh, no. I eat coconuts all the time."

A thought percolated in my mind. If her reaction was

as severe as she claimed, then according to what I had learned from Jack's call to Miss Evanick, it is possible that someone had found a way apply a soy derivative to her skin. But how would... The cream! Cheryl had mentioned that she and the other performers used a cream every day to keep their skin from drying out after wearing that harsh make up. She would have no reason to believe that a moisturizer she had used every day would cause her to have a severe allergic reaction. The problem was, anyone could have meddled with her that cream. I needed to get back to the circus.

Chapter 9

My shift ended in the late afternoon and I rushed out of there before Mr. Stilton had a chance to ask me to stay later. I didn't think Al would be stupid enough to kill Cheryl, despite the fact that he seemed cold about it. There was just no reason for him to murder her, but the owner of the circus was a possibility if she had overheard his plans. Even that didn't make a lot of sense.

I pulled out my phone and dialed Greg.

"Hey, Mel," he said when he answered.

"Are you busy?"

"I'm having to pull a late shift. What do you need?"

"I want to go back to the circus and snoop around."

The phone went silent for a while and I knew he had covered the mouthpiece to talk to his coworkers, before I heard him back on the line. "Unfortunately, I seemed to have used up all my favors. Can it wait until tomorrow?"

I didn't want to wait until the next morning. Anything could happen between now and then. "What if I take Tiny with me?"

"You've already asked him?"

"Yeah." Okay, so I hadn't yet, but I was going to anyway. "And he says he'll do it if you can't."

"All right, but only if he's with you the entire time. I don't like the idea of you going over there alone."

"I'll be fine. And, you're off tomorrow, right?"

"Yeah."

"How about we meet up for lunch when I go on break?"

"Sure thing. And be careful."

I assured him that I would be fine and hung up. Next, I called Tiny and hoped he wouldn't mind coming with me to the circus.

"Yo, Mel."

"Tiny, I have a small favor to ask."

"Name it."

"I need someone to come with me while I go back to the circus and snoop around. I can go myself if you're…"

"Where you at?"

"Just leaving work."

"Be there in 15."

The line went dead. "Cheryl," I whispered into thin air, "if you are around or can hear me, I'm going back to the circus to try and find out who really had you killed."

No response. I didn't expect to receive one. Ghosts were unpredictable. One minute they are with you and the next, they're not. I hoped she had heard me though. She had seemed down the last couple of days.

While I waited for Tiny, I texted Jackie, telling her that I would be home a little late and to not worry. By the time she finished admonishing me through various texts about my insane plan to go back to the circus, the roar of Tiny's bike echoed down the road. He stopped in front of me and handed me a helmet. I knew that I would never get him to ride in the passenger seat of my car, nor would he allow me to just follow him, so I put on the helmet and sat behind him on the bike.

"So, what's the plan?" Tiny asked.

"I need the owner distracted while I search his office."

Tiny grunted and sped off.

With Tiny's way of driving fast, we arrived at the circus within 15 minutes. I didn't know how we would find the owner of the circus or keep him busy, but as it turned out, I didn't have to look very hard to find him. Tiny plowed through the parking area and stopped by a small trailer with a sign that read, "Main Office". I didn't remember it being there, but somehow Tiny had spotted it.

"What is all this?" demanded a man, charging up to us. It had to be the circus owner.

"Uh…" I began, but didn't know what to say to this wrathful man that marched up to me.

Tiny stepped between us, forcing the owner to pause and rethink his approach. "I'm looking for a job."

"We don't need any more performers," replied the owner, his voice much more subdued.

"You need men to take stuff down, don't you?" continued Tiny.

The owner thought about it a moment. "We could use some help with taking down a few of the tents we have. Tonight is our last show."

"I'll take cash," said Tiny, "and the pay can be whatever you feel is a fair rate."

Al walked up to the owner in a hurry. He stopped and glared at me, but one look at Tiny forced him to keep his mouth shut. Instead, he whispered in the owner's ear and the man cursed. I knew it was bad news.

"The fool," hissed the owner.

"Is there a problem?" I asked, trying to sound innocent.

Both the owner and Al ignored me.

"Hey," said Tiny in his usual gruff voice, "she asked you a question."

"Who are you, anyway?" asked the owner and Al's eyes turned toward me, boring into me as though he was trying to learn my innermost secrets.

"His girlfriend," I said. "Isn't that right… sweetie?"

"His girlfriend?" Al asked in a skeptical tone.

"You heard her," Tiny said. "Now do I have a job or don't I?"

"Can you lift 100 pounds?" asked the owner.

"Lift it? Is that a joke?"

"Just answer the question."

"Yeah, I can lift it? Why?"

"One of our performers has suddenly become ill. I need someone who can throw 100 pounds of weights into a ring. If you can do it, I'll pay $100. His performance only lasts about 15 minutes."

"A $100 for 15 minutes of work. Yeah, I'll do it."

"Al will show you what you need."

"Uh, remember," Al said to the owner, "you need to be in that tent tonight."

The owner walked off, grumbling to himself. I couldn't make out what he said, but his sour mood was evident; though, I wondered if there was ever a time when he wasn't in a foul mood.

"This way," said Al.

We followed Al to a small tent, where a few vanity mirrors were, along with trunks containing costumes. He reached in one and pulled out a pair of yellow leotards, complete with sequins. Al handed it to Tiny, giving him a sly look before walking off and disappearing into the tent where the main show was.

"I'm not wearing this," said Tiny as he held the leotards up.

I studied the outfit. It didn't look big enough to fit me, much less him. "I'm sure it will stretch," I said.

Tiny gave me a piercing stare and I knew he wasn't happy about it.

"Come on, please," I begged him. "I need to search the owner's office."

Grimacing, Tiny took the leotards and stepped behind a screen as I stood lookout. I heard the door to the trailer squeak as someone stepped out and marched to the main tent where the cheering onlookers were. I assumed it was the owner, but Tiny's kibitzing as he put on the skintight outfit distracted me.

"You almost ready?" I asked Tiny as I turned back to the screen that he was behind.

"Almost," replied Tiny. "These things are riding up in places that I didn't…"

I tuned out the rest of that statement as it bordered on the realm of too much information.

Tiny stepped out from behind that screen and I burst out laughing. It's a good thing that I didn't have anything to drink, because if I had, I would have spat it all over him. He looked like this walking burst of sunshine with tattoos.

"I will smack you if you don't stop laughing," said Tiny, crossing his beefy arms.

"Sorry," I said, "it's just too funny. Look, I had to dress up as a clown yesterday and get tossed through the air, so I feel your pain." I tried to suppress a giggle, but it came out anyway. Before Tiny could move, I pulled out my phone and snapped a picture, knowing that I would never get another opportunity to do so.

"Hey!" Tiny reached for my phone, but I pulled away. "What are you doing?"

"Texting Elise," I said as I dodged his reach.

"You wouldn't."

"It's just one person—Uh-oh." I looked at the recipients list for the text message I had sent and cringed. Instead of just sending it to Elise, I had accidentally sent it to everyone on my contacts list, which included Detective Shorts. Oh boy. Tiny was going to kill me when he found out, which would be any second.

My phone buzzed with a series of texts coming through.
Jackie: *LOL* 😉
Elise: *OOOOO. Me like.*
Greg: *Do I want to know what you are up to? HA-HA!*

My heart sunk when a message from Detective Shorts appeared on my screen.

I know you're at the circus. Stay put until I get there.

"Mel," said Tiny, turning towards me, "would you mind explaining why I just received a message from Sombrero and the guys, telling me how sexy I look in these leotards?" He held his phone out to me so I could read the text.

"I might have... sort of... maybe sent the picture to everyone by mistake."

"You what?"

I knew Tiny would never forgive me for this, but before he could yell at me any further, Al poked his head out and whistled at us.

"Hey, muscle-man. Get in here now or you can forget about being paid."

Tiny glared at me and I gave him a pleading look. With a grunt, he followed Al into the tent. I peeked through the flap and watched as Al led Tiny to the ring and explained what to do. The owner was there too, watching everything with the same sour expression. I don't think he ever smiled. Knowing I only had moments, I left the tent and hurried over to the trailer.

The door was unlocked, thank goodness, because I didn't feel like trying to pick it, and I let myself inside. I felt my way around until I found a lamp and turned it on. The small, built in table was littered with papers and a laptop in the middle. I picked up a stack of papers and leafed through them. They were newspaper clippings and all of them concerned animal attacks that had taken place in various places. This didn't look good.

I put the clippings down and opened the laptop. The screen flickered to life, making me glad that it had only been in sleep mode and not shut down. I brought up the web browser and looked through the history, finding more websites about animal attacks, with most of them being about tigers, and severe allergic reactions, the causes, and treatment.

I pulled out my phone so that I could take a picture and as I did so, I noticed a green cap buried under some of the paper. I reached for it and pulled out a canister of facial cream. Hadn't Cheryl mentioned that all the performers use such a cream because to the way the makeup dries out their skin? Except, the owner never performed in the ring so far as I knew.

A creak sounded outside the door followed by someone falling down the steps. I turned off the light and peeked out the window, but didn't see anything. There was no movement or voices. I crept to the door and opened it a crack and still didn't see anything, but I did hear a muffled grunt. Opening the door wider and stepping out, I watched as I realized who had shown up. "Cheryl?"

"It's me," she replied as a faint outline of her appeared. "Sorry I'm late."

"What are you doing on the ground?"

"These steps are a bit unsteady and I tripped."

Tripped? How can a ghost trip? I ignored the question and I remembered how Cheryl had a way of knocking things over to begin with.

I pulled out my phone to call Detective Shorts when a gruff voice stopped me.

"What are you doing here?" it demanded.

Turning away from Cheryl, I came face to face with the owner of the circus and he was not happy to see me and it was at this point that I realized that I still held the canister of facial cream. "Nothing," I said, but I knew he saw right through me.

"Get out of there now!" He grabbed my arm and yanked me off the stairs, but Cheryl saw it and tackled him. It was the first time I had seen her do such a thing. In the commotion, I lost my grip on the canister of cream and it flew through the air, landing by a pair of shoes that belonged to Detective Shorts.

"What is going on here?" demanded Detective Shorts.

"This woman broke into my trailer," the owner said.

Detective Shorts gave me a disapproving look.

"I want her arrested," said the owner.

"I will deal with her later. In the meantime, I have a warrant to search your trailer." Detective Shorts pulled out a rectangular piece of paper and handed it to the owner of the circus who looked it over, the frown on his face increasing with each passing second.

"This is ridiculous!" shouted the owner.

In answer to his outburst, Detective Shorts picked up the cream with a gloved hand and handed it to an officer who placed it in a plastic evidence bag. He waved the other officers with him to enter the trailer.

"Thanks," I whispered to Cheryl when no one seemed to be paying attention to me.

"No problem." Her voice sounded sullen.

"What's wrong?"

"Nothing, it's just… I just remembered that the people I had heard arguing… well, one was a man and one was a woman."

"Miss Summers?" Detective Shorts waved me over, interrupting my conversation with Cheryl, as Tiny walked up to us; he had thrown his jacket on over his circus outfit. "Didn't I tell you to stay put?"

"You might have said something like that," I replied. I looked around for Cheryl, but she had vanished, not liking all of the extra people around.

"So, why are you here?"

"Well…"

"Sir," one of the uniformed officers walked up, interrupting us for which I was very thankful, "we found all of these and this laptop has some interesting things on it."

Detective Shorts glanced at the newspaper clippings and his brows furrowed.

"That laptop isn't mine!" screamed the circus owner as the detective placed him under arrest.

Once the man had been put in a police cruiser, the detective came up to me. "Go home," he said. "If I catch you here again, I will arrest you for trespassing."

"I'll make sure she goes home," said Tiny.

Detective Shorts glanced at him, his face unreadable, saying, "Yellow is not your color."

Tiny's cheeks reddened and he glowered at me.

"I'm sorry," I said.

"Let's go."

Tiny led me away from the scene as the police tore apart the circus owner's trailer and to his bike. I put the helmet he handed me on, sat behind him, and we rode off. It would be a long while before he would be able to live down the yellow leotards and before he forgave me for accidentally texting everyone the picture I took of him in them.

Chapter 10

The next morning was like any other. I woke up late and hurried around as I attempted to simultaneously dress, chug a cup of coffee, and down a bowl of cereal. All I ended up doing was spilling coffee on my pants and getting bits of cereal in my bra, which resulted in me having to change. The joys of adulthood.

I squeaked into the Candle Shoppe right at nine, just in time to hear—

"Mel!"

Tammy slammed into me, giving me such a tight squeeze that I thought my lungs would be pushed up my throat and out my mouth. When she let go, I heaved in a mouthful of air, thankful that I could still breathe.

"Nice to see you too," I said to her as I headed out to the main storeroom and its early morning shoppers.

"I heard you caught the killer!"

I hushed her as a few heads turned our way. "It would seem so."

For once, Tammy realized that her exuberant nature needed to be toned down—we didn't need the few customers in the store to think that we spent our days discussing murder—and whispered to me, "I can't believe it was the owner."

Though the evidence had been there, I had a hard time believing it as well. The evidence all seemed circumstantial, but that didn't always mean innocent. I remembered Randall and how the evidence against him had seemed circumstantial, but it turned out that he had committed murder. "It would seem so," I said to Tammy, hoping that she would get back to work and leave me alone, but no such luck.

Tammy pulled out her phone and thrust it in front of my face. "I recorded your act the other day. Look! You have over 200,000 views."

I clenched my fists as I watched the clown version of myself get pushed around, water thrown in my face, and forced to jump off a diving board and onto a trampoline where I flew through the air like the human version of a flying pig, and crashed into the ground amidst a laughing and cheering crowd. I could have killed her. "Tammy, please tell me you didn't."

Her face shook as her smile grew wider. "I posted it the moment I left you guys at the circus. It's a web sensation. You're famous, Mel!"

Tammy's innocent look conveyed that she never thought that posting the video of me making a fool out of myself might be overstepping her bounds; and the damage had been done.

"Next time," I said to her, "ask me before you post a video of me on the web. What if Mr. Stilton sees it?"

Her face fell. She hadn't thought of that. Though, I didn't think my boss spent much time on the web browsing through senseless videos on the internet either.

"I didn't mean to upset you. I'm still just a little sore from that day."

"Ice packs work wonders. Or heating pads. I have one in my car I can—"

"That's okay, but thanks for the offer."

I noticed Cheryl standing in a corner, watching us, while playing with her hair and trying to not be seen. Why hadn't she moved on? The police were confident that the man who had murdered her had been caught.

"Miss," said a customer, "may I get some help, please?"

"Yes, I'll be right there." I glanced back at where Cheryl had been, but she had gone and an empty feeling filled my stomach. What if finding the one who had murdered her was not the one thing that would bring her peace in the afterlife?

I didn't have time to worry about Cheryl, but made a mental note to try calling her parents again, guessing that it was the reason for her remaining, and followed the woman who had asked for assistance. "How may I help you?" I said to her.

"Can you tell me anything about these warmers?"

She pointed a boney finger at the shelf of scented oil warmers that we had.

"Well, they are fairly easy to use. You put a little bit of scented oil"—I grabbed the small bottle of oil we used when demonstrating the warmers—"in here like this and turn on the warmer. The heat from the tiny bulb warms the oil which fills the area with a pleasant scent."

"And is it safe to leave alone for hours at a time?"

"Yes, and it has an automatic shut off, which turns it off in four hours if no one touches it."

"Would it work in the bathroom?"

"Pardon?"

"I need something that I can place in the main bathroom of my home. Every time my husband gets through doing his business in there, it smells worse than an outhouse."

Well, that was a new one. "We have some more compact warmers over here that you can place in a small corner. It will be out of the way, but should help keep your bathroom smelling fresh."

"Then I'll take two."

"Two?"

"Well, we have two bathrooms in total and when we both eat burritos it can…"

"I'll wrap them up for you," I interrupted her as the conversation had bordered on the TMI department. "Are there any particular scented oils you would like included?"

"Oh, just give me whatever the most popular one is." She dug around in her briefcase-sized purse for her wallet.

After I had packed the warmers in boxes, and wrapped

them in paper for extra protection, I snatched two bottles of the cinnamon vanilla and honeydew oils. They were our more popular scents and weren't overpowering.

"Only four bottles of your oils?" The woman gave me a disbelieving look.

"One bottle last about a month."

"You better put in five more."

How bad were their episodes in the bathroom? Five more bottles of scented oil would last them half a year. How much was... you know what? I didn't want to know. I snatched five more bottles of our oils, not paying attention to the particular scent, and I didn't think she cared, and wrapped them in paper before placing them in a paper bag.

"How much?" she asked, holding out a wad of $20 bills.

"$114.93."

She handed me $120.00 and I counted out her change, but before I could hand it to her, she shoved the money back into my hands.

"Keep it."

"It's..."

"Oh, you keep it as a tip. I remember working in a flower shop back in my youth. I worked hard and always appreciated the times people gave me a tip. So you keep that."

"Um... thanks."

I watched as the woman walked through the door with her bundle and after she had disappeared from sight, I put the change she had refused in the donation box to the children's hospital that we kept on the counter. I didn't need it.

The rest of the morning passed quickly without any more interesting characters. I was glad when noontime rolled around and I could take my lunch. I texted Greg, asking him if he wanted to grab a quick bite before I had to be back at work and he replied back, saying that he'd love to.

"Want to go to lunch together?" Tammy asked me just as I put my phone away.

"I just made plans with Greg."

A disappointed look crossed her face. I know that Jackie and I are not always very welcoming around Tammy; her personality is a bit much to handle, but the deflated look on her face tugged at my conscience.

"Maybe tomorrow? I'm sorry, Tammy. If you had asked a moment earlier then I would have liked to, but Greg and I haven't..."

"I understand."

"Are you Mellow Summers?"

Tammy and I both turned with a start at the soft voice of the newcomer, whom neither of us had noticed.

"Tomorrow, then," said Tammy as she left.

I waved at her and faced the familiar-looking woman before me. "Yes, I'm Mellow Summers."

"Can we talk? In private."

I checked my watch and decided that I had a few minutes to spare. "Sure."

I led her through the doors and out on the sidewalk. We could at least talk and walk to the restaurant where I was to meet Greg.

"It's terrible, what happened. I can't believe that the owner would have done that to Cheryl," said the woman.

"Well, it looks as though he did do it, though I have no reason why."

"Does that matter?" the woman asked.

I studied her a moment and it clicked as to where I had seen her before and why she looked so familiar. She was the woman who had lost her temper, when I had gone to the circus with Jackie and Greg disguised as a clown, and a tray full of makeup had fallen. I had passed her off as rude, but perhaps she was just upset by Cheryl's death, who still remained elusive.

"To me it does."

The woman gave me a quizzical look before shaking it off and resuming her saddened demeanor. "But the police said that they had all the evidence they needed to prosecute."

True, there was more than enough there for the prosecuting attorney to make a case, but that still didn't explain how he had managed to get to the tiger's cage and open it, without anyone noticing. He also had a genuine look of surprise and disgust that someone would insinuate that he had murdered someone. Something was missing, and I couldn't let it go. I jerked my head, thinking that I had seen a bit of glitter and a wisp of Cheryl's hair, but she had gone by the time I had turned around.

"What's wrong?" asked the woman.

"Nothing," I said.

"You don't think he did it."

Was I that obvious? "It doesn't matter. The police believe they have the right guy and they have enough evidence"—I looked at my watch—"and I need to go, or I'll be late."

I stared to leave, but the woman stopped me with her next statement.

"You could be right."

What? Now she thinks I might be correct about my misgivings? "Say again?"

"I found something. I didn't think much of it until now, but it's back at the circus."

"What did you find?"

The woman looked around as though she were nervous before closing the distance and whispering, "It's best if I show you."

"Show me?"

"It's back there at the circus. I can't just bring it here, but if you really think that he didn't do it, then I think you ought to see this. It could prove one way or the other."

A part of me told me to walk away, but another part had to know what she had. If the circus owner hadn't done it, then I had to know who did for Cheryl's sake and to keep an innocent man from going to jail. "All right," I agreed. "My car is down that way."

"Mine's right here. Well, it really belongs to the circus, but we're allow to borrow it if we need to."

The fact that we had been walking to her car the whole time seemed odd to me, but my curiosity overruled all common sense, like it always did. I texted Greg, but put Detective Shorts as the second recipient of the message, telling him that I would be a few minutes late because someone from the circus said they had information about the case, but to go ahead and order for the both of us. As I got into the car, something tugged on my arm, but I couldn't see who it was. "Cheryl?" I whispered, hoping the woman wouldn't hear, but received no answer. Where was she?

Within minutes of us leaving, my phone buzzed. It was a message from Detective Shorts. *Stay where you are.*

Too late, I texted back.

"Who was that?" asked the woman.

"Just my boyfriend. I was supposed to meet him for lunch. He's just checking in to see why I'm late. This won't take too long will it?"

"No, we're here now."

My phone slipped from my hand as I tried to put it back in my purse and plopped on the floor of the car. As I reached down to pick it up, I noticed a small bottle nestled in the pocket on the side of the door. I moved my hand so that I could grab it while pretending to pick up my phone. Soybean oil? What would she be doing with a small bottle of soybean oil? And didn't Cheryl say that she had a severe reaction to anything with soy in it?

"You okay down there?" the woman asked as we pulled into the circus parking area.

"Fine. Just dropped my phone."

I put the bottle of oil back and snatched my phone. When I glanced out the car window, I almost gasped. The area that had once been filled with tents, trailers, trucks, cars, crates, and people dressed in ostentatious garb looked almost barren. The tents were missing, except for one or two that people were busy taking down, and most of the props had been packed away.

"You guys pack up quick," I commented.

"Yeah, well with the owner being arrested, Al decided it was best we leave. Worn out our welcome, you know."

The woman parked the car near a trailer, with its overhang still extended.

My phone buzzed as I stepped out of the car. "Hi, Greg," I said when I answered.

"Mel, it's Jack."

"I know."

"You're in trouble again, aren't you?"

"You could say that," I turned toward the woman and she had pulled a gun on me.

"Hang up the phone," she said.

I pressed the mute button on my phone instead of the end call button, and put it in my pocket. "Why?"

"People talk, you know. After the death of that stupid girl, some spoke about a town psychic who never rests until the case is solved. I passed it off as a joke at first, but then you and your friends kept showing up here. Your clown disguise fooled no one. And then I found this."

She tossed an old newspaper article at me, one of the ones that Jillian Modsen had written.

"So what's your plan? You're going to kill me?"

"I killed Cheryl already. It wouldn't be hard to stuff your body into one these trunks and dispose of it on the road. It'd be a long time before anyone found you."

"But why kill Cheryl?" It dawned on me. Cheryl had mentioned that she had overheard a woman arguing with the owner, not a man, which ruled out Al. "You're the woman. The one she overheard."

"The stupid snoop. Yeah, she overheard me arguing with the owner, or I should say my father."

Father? When did that happen?

"My mother was once a circus performer, same as the owner here. They had a fling, but he broke it off when he learned she was pregnant. I never knew about my father until a few years ago. So, I looked him up."

I heard something move, but didn't know what and I didn't want to turn away from the woman with the gun. "And what, you thought he would just give this to you?"

"I had hoped. You see, I did some digging about the traveling circus and its popularity in certain areas. I knew how I could make this a huge success and even had some investors lined up, but my father refused to go along with it. He wanted to sell it—be done with it—but he refused to sell to me. I'm his daughter! I have every right to this!"

"Did anyone else know that you were…"

"No, not until that night when the klutzy Cheryl overheard us arguing. I knew she had a severe allergy to soybean oil. Most everyone here did. And with the research I had done about animal attacks, I knew most people wouldn't question it. So, I put some soybean oil in her facial cream, but before I did that, I dressed like her and visited that stupid tiger and I poked it and threw things at it to get it mad. It worked. And right before her performance that day, I made sure that the lock on the tiger's cage hadn't latched and that the covering was pulled back just enough so he would see her as she walked past. It worked."

"I don't see how killing her solved anything."

"I had originally planned on murdering my father, but she had overheard me threaten him."

"Is it true?" said a weepy voice. Neither of us had noticed Ellie approach. She must have seen us drive up and came over, overhearing everything. "You killed Cheryl?"

"I guess you will have company in that trunk."

A crowbar floated through the air, heading for the woman, but it faltered, and I knew Cheryl had to have tripped over her own feet as it smashed into the line holding up the overhang, which snapped, dropping the overhang onto the woman.

"Dang it!" yelled Cheryl, though she remained invisible. "Mel!"

Tammy? What was she doing here?

I ignored Tammy's outburst. The moment the overhang fell, I grabbed Ellie and shoved her to the other side of the trailer away from the commotion, but I needn't have bothered. A gunshot rang out, stopping everyone. As I looked up, Detective Shorts had his gun out and was surrounded by officers.

"Take that woman into custody," he ordered, and two officers rushed to the woman on the ground and put her wrists in zip ties, but before they hauled her away, Ellie rushed up to her and punched her in the face.

Others from the circus surrounded us, wondering what the commotion was all about, just as a great weight slammed into me knocking me to the ground.

"Mel! Are you all right?"

"I'm fine, Tammy. Do you mind getting off me?"

"Oh, sorry." Tammy stood up, allowing me to regain my feet.

"What are you doing here?"

"Um… nothing."

Before I could get anymore answers from Tammy, Detective Shorts walked up, interrupting us. "I got your message. Will there ever be a time when you actually listen to me and stay out of it?"

I didn't answer. What was the point? He knew I wouldn't.

"Do you need a ride home?"

"Oh, I can take her!" Tammy jumped up and down, the ruffled balls on her socks bounced with each movement.

"It's settled then."

"Mel!" Cheryl whispered when the Detective had left and Tammy wasn't paying attention.

I hurried over to her. She had somehow gotten her foot caught in some rope. I'm not sure how she had managed it, but I reached down and untangled it for her.

"Thanks," she whispered.

"Actually, I should be thanking you. You saved our lives."

Cheryl smiled and disappeared.

Ellie joined her family after the police had led the woman away and I left with Tammy, still wondering why she was there in the first place. I found out the moment we reached her car and a silhouette of ears greeted me.

"What is the tiger doing in the backseat of your car?" I asked Tammy.

She fiddled with her fingers and shifted from foot to foot. "Well. I… I couldn't just let them take him. He needs a good home and I can't just let them put him down."

"I don't think they're going to be doing that now that they have the real murderer."

Tammy pouted.

"Rocky!" The tiger trainer's voice echoed throughout the compound and I knew just what to do.

I marched to the car door, opened it, and let the tiger out. The animal jumped to the ground and bounded over to the trainer, who knelt and gave him a giant hug, glad to have found his friend again, after having gone missing for the second time.

"I wanted to keep him," whined Tammy.

"But he already has an owner. And why aren't you back at work?"

"I took an extended lunch break so that I could—"

"Kidnap the tiger for a second time?"

Tammy hung her head. I checked my watch, realizing that my lunch break was over. "We should get back."

We got in her car and left the scene of flashing lights and patrolling officers behind, while I called Greg to apologize for missing lunch.

Chapter 11

"Jackie," I said through her bedroom door, "Greg and I are ready."

"In a minute!"

I sighed as I walked back to the living room where Greg waited, looking sharp in his button up sage green shirt and Khaki pants.

"We're going to be late to the memorial," he said, tapping his watch.

"You know Jackie. She has to look perfect."

Ellie had invited us to a memorial service for Cheryl and we had accepted, hoping that it would give Cheryl some sort of peace.

"Jackie, we're going to be late!" I called to her.

"I'm coming!" She stepped out of her room in a huff. "I couldn't find any shoes that matched this skirt."

I gave her a reproachful look, trying not to laugh at her inherent need to have her clothes match. I opened the door to leave, but stopped when I found a woman with salt and pepper hair standing there. Her sorrowful face told me that she was not there by accident.

"May I help you?" I asked her.

"I'm looking for a Mellow Summers."

"That's me."

"I'm Cheryl's mother. You had called a few days ago about her..."

"I'll meet you guys at the car," I said to both Greg and Jackie before turning back to the woman. "Do you want to come in?"

"No," said Cheryl's mother. "I know that my husband was a bit rude when you called. At first, I couldn't believe that such a thing could have happened and thought it was a prank, but then I saw this." She pulled out her phone with an article about the tiger mauling at the circus. "I knew, then, that you were no crank call. Did you know her well? Did she suffer?"

"I don't think she did, and I didn't know her very well, I'm afraid. Would you like to come to the service? There will be people there who knew her for the last few years, perhaps they can..."

"Yes, that would be nice. I'm sorry that my husband isn't here. He is very stubborn and when he makes up his mind, there is no changing it."

"It's okay. You can ride with us."

I locked the door and led Cheryl's mother down the hall and to the parking garage. Along the way, I saw Cheryl standing next to a light. She and I locked eyes, before she smiled and vanished. I guess now she had found some peace.

Look for book 12 in the series

Hickory, Dickory Dock, The Dwarf In The Clock

Coming Soon

About the Author

Janet McNulty currently lives in West Virginia where she continues to work on the Mellow Summers Series. She began the series two years ago as a fluke, but liked writing it so much, that she decided to stick with it.

Besides writing paranormal mysteries, Ms. McNulty has also accomplished success in other genres. She has a fantasy saga (*Legends Lost*) published under the name of Nova Rose and a new dystopian trilogy (*Dystopia*) and acience fiction series (*Solaris Saga*) as well. Ms. McNulty once referred to herself as an author who is "a little something for everyone."

She is currently busy working on the next Mellow Summers book.

Of course, writing is not the only passion in her life and every author needs some down time. When she isn't working on her books, Ms. McNulty enjoys reading and just poking around in her garden.

More by Janet McNulty

The Mellow Summers Series

Sugar And Spice And Not So Nice
Frogs, Snails, And A Lot Of Wails
An Apple A Day Keeps Murder Away
Three Little Ghosts
Oh Holy Ghost
Where Trouble Roams
Two Ghosts Haunt A Grove
Trick Or Treat Or Murder
Roses Are Red…He's Dead
Double, Double, Nothing But Trouble
Ring Around The Rosy, Not Another Ghosty

Mellow Summers moves to Vermont to attend college, accompanied by her friend Jackie. They soon find themselves running into ghosts and one mystery after another.

The Solaris Saga

Solaris Seethes
Solaris Seeks
Solaris Strays
Solaris Soars

Every myth has a beginning.

After escaping the destruction of her home planet, Lanyr, with the help of the mysterious Solaris, Rynah must put her faith in an ancient legend. Never one to believe in stories and legends, she is forced to follow the ancient tales of her people: tales that also seem to predict her current situation.

Forced to unite with four unlikely heroes from an unknown planet (the philosopher, the warrior, the lover, the inventor) in order to save the Lanyran people, Rynah and Solaris embark on an adventure that will shatter everything Rynah once believed.

The Legends Lost Series

Published under Nova Rose

Tesnayr
Amborese
Galdin

Enter the Lands of Tesnayr and join on an epic fantasy adventure that spans over 1,500 years.

Begin with Tesnayr, the first king of the five lands as he unites the against a savage foe bent on their destruction.

Next, Join Amborese as she fights reclaim the throne after her family was forced to flee from it.

Thinking peace has finally entered the land, follow Galdin as he returns to Tesnayr to find it greatly hanged. Barbarians, led by a mysterious sorcerer, burn and destroy as they go. And only Galdin can stop them if he chooses to accept his fate.

Visit www.legendslosttrilogy.com to learn more about the Legends Lost Trilogy.

The Dystopia Trilogy

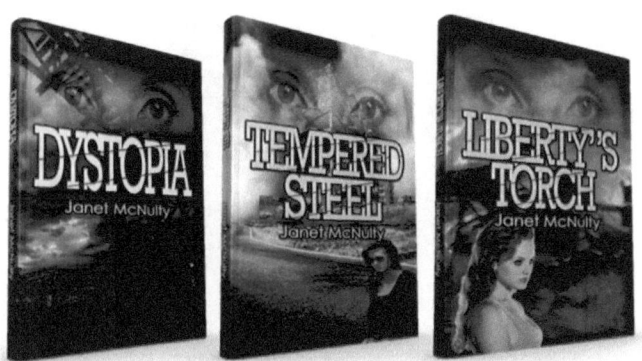

Dystopia (Book 1)
Tempered Steel (Book 2)
Liberty's Torch (Book 3)

**Imagine living in a world where
everything you do is controlled.**

Dana Ginary lives in a world where every aspect of her life is controlled by the Dystopian Government. Forced to work in Waste Management, her life becomes a nightmare with hunger and survival is her only constant. Before she knows it, she is caught up in a resistance movement and exiled from Dystopia, forced to find her way in the barren wastelands. While there, she must learn to live independently and discover how far she is willing to go to live and achieve freedom.

Grandpa's Stories

  My grandfather grew up in Arizona during the 1920s and 1930s. One week after the attack on Pearl Harbor he joined the Navy. During the summer of 2012, my mother visited him and recorded his stories about growing up, World War II, and his time as an employee at the Pacific Bell Telephone Company. This is the history of the 20th century as he lived it. These recordings make up this book. These are his words.